The Turning of the Tide

Or, Radcliffe Rich and ?

Elijah Kellogg

Alpha Editions

This edition published in 2024

ISBN : 9789362514479

Design and Setting By
Alpha Editions
www.alphaedis.com
Email - info@alphaedis.com

Contents

PREFACE.

A distinguished professor of Mathematics in a New England college was wont to remark to the Freshman class when meeting them for the first time at recitation, "that every person is as lazy as he can be." However we may demur to this sweeping assertion, it is doubtless true that more persons fail in life through indolence and the absence of appropriate and wholesome stimulus than from lack of capacity to become useful and even distinguished.

Misfortune, undesirable as it may seem, nevertheless furnishes an effective test of character, for, while the effeminate nature of lax fibre crumbles and is disintegrated beneath the pressure, the manlier spirit, like Dannemora iron, defies the fury of the furnace, and even beneath the hammer, gathers both temper and tenacity.

How great the change produced in a Scotch pebble, taken from the banks of a Highland lake, when the wheel of the lapidary has brought out the hues, and it appears what it really is, a gem; thus the thrill of sudden calamity, the sharp anguish that makes the blood spring from the lip have often supplied both object and motive to many a spirit that (capacious of better things) was fast becoming honeycombed by the rust of luxury and indolence, and has developed gifts of which even the possessor was unconscious.

The TURNING OF THE TIDE places before our readers this entire process in the person of RADCLIFFE RICH, from the rude awakening, the moment when the half-benumbed faculties rally for the mastery, to the stern conflict and the hard-won victory.

CHAPTER I.
THE SMITH OF THE WILDERNESS.

With Rich, the chum and friend of Morton, and who, animated by the contagion of a noble example, became his rival in rank as a scholar and in all athletic sports, his companion in labor, and between whom, though neck and neck in the pursuit of those college honors that each most highly prized, there was never a shadow of jealousy or distrust, while their sympathies met and mingled like fibres of a kindred root, drawing their nutriment from a common soil,—with Rich, refined in all his tastes, of delicate sensibilities, and a playful humor that never stung, sunny tempered, generous, companionable, yet firm in principle as a granite shaft, and whom all Radcliffe idolized, our constant readers are already well acquainted; but the exigencies of this story, and the necessity of imparting information both to them and others, render it imperative that we should speak more definitely respecting his family and home life, to which we have heretofore barely alluded; indeed, we are not aware that we have ever distinguished him by any other name than that of Richardson, and much more frequently made use of the college term, Rich.

His grandfather, with ten other young married men, first broke ground in our hero's native town, then a wilderness, and built their camps on the borders of a stream heavily timbered, soon after the formation of the federal government with Washington as president. They were, with a single exception, poor, having taken up their abode in the wilderness because they wanted a home, and could buy the wild land for ten cents per acre. Full of enterprise, and strong in limb, this little community felt themselves equal to the struggle. They had as yet neither sawmill nor gristmill, though a noble stream fell over the rocks close to their doors, but pounded the corn they raised on burns in large mortars, or went in canoes eleven miles to mill, to a village farther down the stream, where they likewise procured salt. There were neither roads nor horses in the clearing, and at first everything was brought through the woods, in the winter on men's shoulders, walking on snow-shoes, and in summer in canoes or on rafts up the river.

They were accustomed to put the grain and corn belonging to several neighbors into a large canoe, and thus take it down the river to the mill. At length a road was spotted through the woods to the village—that is, a piece of bark and wood was taken off the side of trees with an axe, for a guide to the traveler. The path was crooked, going through those portions of the forest that were thinnest, and winding around obstacles. Occasionally a tree that stood very much in the way was cut, and a log flung across some gully, brook, or mire.

In the early part of winter, when the brooks and swamps were frozen, and the snow deep enough to cover, in some measure, the windfalls, and fill the ravines, and at other times in the latter part of it, when the crust would bear light cattle, they went through the woods with oxen to mill, improved the occasion to obtain articles of absolute necessity, and whenever their stock of bread-stuff fell short, had recourse to the mortar.

At first it was a bitter struggle for existence; the land was covered with a dense forest, and there was neither pasture for cattle in the summer, nor hay to keep them through the winter. In this condition of things, they managed to keep a few cattle by cutting the wild grass that grew in the swamp and along the banks of the river, and felling yellow birch and maple trees in summer for browse. By dint of patient labor, their circumstances improved from year to year; more land was cleared, their stock of cattle increased with the increase of hay and pasture, and they began to keep sheep and horses, to make staves and shingles, cut logs and drive them down the river in spring, and beech withes to bind loads and rafts were exchanged for chains.

Cattle and horses were now to be shod, and they began to feel greatly the need of a blacksmith. If a chain or axe was broken, a horse or yoke of oxen to be shod, there was no smith nearer than eleven miles, and no road except a bridle-path through spotted trees. Previous to this, they had worked their oxen without shoes, and horses were only shod forward. But now they wanted to haul logs and shingles on the ice of the river, and they must be shod. They were in great need of a smith, and yet there was not work sufficient to afford a blacksmith constant employment, and consequently, a living. But there was money in the logs and shingles, and necessity sharpens invention. They hired John Drew, the smith at the village, to come in the fall, just before the river shut up, bringing horse-shoes, ox-shoes, nails, and his tools. He went round from house to house, the oxen were cast on the barn floors, and the shoes put on. Thus they managed, feeling more and more the want of a smith. Richardson was possessed of remarkable mechanical ability, and was what is termed a handy man—a great thing in the woods. He had a few carpenters' tools, made ox-yokes, and sleds for himself and neighbors. At length a cart road was made through the woods, and Richardson built the first, and for some time the only, pair of wheels in the clearing. Surrounded by a young and rapidly increasing family, necessity led him to improve to the utmost every talent he was conscious of possessing.

On the 10th of January, some two years before the road was made, he went, in behalf of himself and the little community, to the village, through the woods, with an ox-team, carrying corn and grain to be ground. He also carried plough-irons to be new laid, chains to be mended, axes to be new "laid" or "upset," and orders for some to be manufactured. In order to get the large grist ground, and the iron work done, he was obliged to remain three days. While watching the smith at his work, the idea occurred to him that he could work with iron as well as wood. All the way home he brooded over it, till the idea took entire possession of him, and that long wilderness road never seemed so short before. After a while he opened his mind to his wife, who encouraged him to make the attempt. But he had no money to buy either iron or tools, and iron in those days was difficult to obtain, and high in price, being nearly all imported. It seemed a hopeless undertaking; still he could not banish the thought from his mind. It haunted him; lay down with him at night, and rose up with him in the morning. One day he broke a chain in the woods; he had but two. The next day came a snow storm, affording leisure. The smith was eleven miles off. He could not do his work without the chain, and resolved to try to mend it by welding again the broken link he had saved. He made a great fire in the kitchen, and put in the iron. The kitchen tongs served to hold, a nail hammer to work it, and a flat stone for an anvil. To his great mortification, he found that although he could heat it to redness, he could not make it hot enough, with a wood fire, to weld. He put wood in the oven, stopped the draft, and burnt it to coal; but even with charcoal he did not succeed at first in obtaining a welding heat. His wife, who was looking on with the greatest interest, suggested the use of the kitchen bellows, and by their aid he partially succeeded.

His next attempt was to mend the staple of an ox-yoke. This was much more difficult, as the iron was larger, and he had nothing to bend it over. But after several trials, he at length accomplished his purpose. It was supper time when William Richardson struck the last blow upon the staple, and put it into the yoke. When the meal was finished, and Mrs. Richardson had washed the dishes, and put the children to bed, she sat down to her cards, with a basket of wool beside her, while the father of the family, having taken off his shoes, and hung his buskins in the corner to dry, sat with folded arms, looking intently upon the glowing coals. No sound was heard save the crackling of the fire, the rasping of a solitary wood-worm that was boring into a log of the walls, and the sound of the cards as the good wife plied her labor.

"Well, wife," said Richardson, at length, starting from his reverie, and flinging fresh fuel on the fire, "what do you think of it?"

"Think of what, William?"

"Why, of my day's work, and this blacksmithing. Don't you think I'd better fling the stone into the river and give it up? All I have done this blessed day, besides taking care of the cattle, is to mend that staple—a thing John Drew would have done in fifteen minutes."

"No, he wouldn't, for if he had no better tools than you, he wouldn't have thought he could do it at all. I think it is the best day's work you ever did in your life."

"O, Susan, how do you make that out? You just say that because you know I feel a little down in the mouth; not because you really think so."

"Yes, husband, I really think so; and you will, if you look at it right. You must expect to creep before you can walk. You couldn't have got along without that chain, and would have been obliged to travel twenty-two miles through the woods on snow-shoes, with that chain on your back, in order to get it mended, and a half bushel of corn besides on your shoulder to pay John Drew for doing it; for we've got no money. It would have been the same with the staple. You couldn't have worked your oxen without it, and would have been forced to leave your work in fair weather, for you could not have gone in a storm. Now, you have done it yourself, in stormy days, when you couldn't have done much else, saved your corn, yourself all that travel, and, more than that, found out that you can work iron whenever you can get the tools to do it with."

"I don't know but you are right, wife; but how am I to get either the tools or the iron without money? I can't barter corn for iron, and John Drew has so much produce brought to him now that he is loath to take any more; says his house is full of corn, grain, meat, potatoes, and cloth, butter and eggs, and he can't get *money* enough to pay his taxes."

"I think there will be some way provided. We had nothing when we came here but the clothes on our backs and twenty dollars in money; had to run in debt for our land. Now we've nearly paid for the land, we cut hay, keep quite a stock of cattle and sheep, have but seldom been put to it for bread, and have a warm, comfortable house, if it is a log one, and the children are warm clothed."

"You always look on the bright side, Sue."

"I think that's the best side to look on."

We would inform our readers that the house Sue thought so comfortable was built of rough logs, the crevices stuffed with moss and clay, had but two rooms in it, the partition between them being blankets hung up. The fireplace and oven were built of rough stones, and the chimney of sticks of wood laid in clay (to prevent their taking fire from sparks), that, as it fell off, was renewed from time to time.

"I could buy tools with the money I shall get for logs that I cut this winter, didn't I want every cent of it to turn in towards paying for the land. I'm half a mind to take a little. If I only had a hammer, a punch, something to cut iron with, and a pair of tongs to hold it, I could mend my own chains and other things, save something, be learning all the time, and, after we pay for the land, I could get more tools."

"I never would do that, husband. If we must take that money for anything, let us take it for the school. They are going to have a school at Montague's the latter part of the winter."

This man had three rooms in his house, and it was built of hewn timber, in one of which the school was to be kept. Richardson and his wife had received a good common school education, and were anxious that their children should not grow up in ignorance.

CHAPTER II.
THE FIRST MONEY.

From the preceding chapter our readers will perceive the value of iron, and also the importance to the community of the mechanic who is able to work it. We would invite them to reflect upon some facts that may seem incredible to them at first view. A boy who has no disposition to reflect is not much of a boy, and when grown, will only be a servant to those who do.

Iron is far more valuable than gold, and the blacksmith than the jeweler, for the same reason that bread is worth more than diamonds, and water than silver. Gold has a very great representative value in civilized society, where iron is abundant, and it will buy iron, and is an equivalent for the work of the smith; but it is only because men have agreed to make it so. Whereas iron has a value in itself considered. It fells the forest, tills the soil, annihilates time and distance, and underlies the whole economy of domestic life; for our readers will bear in mind that steel is only another form of iron.

The value iron acquires under the hammer is something wonderful. It is said that a bar of iron worth $5 is worth $10.50 when made into horse-shoes, $55 when made into needles, $3,285 made into penknife blades, $29,480 in shirt buttons, and $250,000, in balance springs of watches. Boys may, from this, see what labor is worth, and learn to value and respect it, for it is the labor the mind put into the iron that so increases its value. Consider what would be the result if there were no iron.

A boy might search long to find a better subject for his theme than iron and its uses, or one the treatment of which would be more instructive to himself. The showers of sparks you see pouring out of a blacksmith's chimney, at times, of an evening when he is pressed with work, and forgets the ten-hour system, have a language to a reflecting mind; they mean power, progress, the plough, the telegraph, the mariner's compass, and the sword.

We have taken advantage of a pause in the conversation, during which William Richardson resumed his reverie, and his wife plied her cards, to make this digression. At length the mother laid her cards into the basket of wool, and folding her hands in her lap, remained a few moments wrapped in thought. She then said,—

"Husband, I feel so sure that good will come of this, that it will be, in the end, the best thing for us all (for I know you can do whatever you put your hand to), that I am willing to undergo almost anything to bring it about. There are three articles that will always sell at the store for half cash and half goods—butter, woollen cloth, and linen yarn. I will sell what we have to get your tools, and, perhaps, a little iron."

"Susan, what did you make this cloth for, and what shape is it in?"

"There's a piece of fulled cloth that I meant to make clothes of for you and the boys, some that I wove for a gown for myself and the girls, and some blanket stuff."

"I won't take it; I won't take the clothes from your back and the children's if I never have any tools: the butter, I suppose, you have laid down for winter, and the blankets are needed for the children's beds."

"Yes, you must take it; if you can work iron, we shall have the house as full of butter, meat, and cloth as John Drew's is."

"But we can't get along without these things."

"We can if we only *think* so. We can put some brush on the children's beds, over the clothes,—hemlock brush over a few clothes is real warm,—then, when it is very cold, we can leave a large fire when we go to bed, and you can get up at twelve o'clock and put on wood. The children can get along with their old clothes, and I with mine; there's nobody to look at us here. We have pork enough, and can do without butter till we can make some. One of the cows calves in March. I meant to have made some towels of the linen yarn, but tow will do just as well."

"Susan, I think a man must be made of poor material who could be discouraged with a wife like you."

"Mother always used to say, 'Think you can do a thing, and it's half done.'"

The sledding was now good, and Richardson, engaged in hauling logs to the river, had no leisure to meddle with iron; he, however, at odd moments, when the cattle were eating, and on stormy days, made preparation in anticipation of the future.

Near to his house stood the stump of a pine tree that had been cut when the snow was deep, and was higher than usual. Around this he built a log camp, in such a manner as to bring the stump on one side of the camp. The water was low in the river, and where it fell over the rocks, and by shovelling away the snow, he found a stone of sufficient size, hardness, and the right shape, for an anvil. Levelling the top of the stump, he made a cavity in it to receive the stone, and secured it firmly in its bed. This was much superior to a stone on the kitchen hearth, and would bear any blows that could be given with a hand-hammer. There was not a board or plank within eleven miles by land, and thirteen by the river. He flattened some pine saplings, and built up a pen, nearly square, for his forge, found a place in the swamp where the soil was not frozen, and obtained earth to fill it. By cutting through the frozen ground at the bank of the river, he obtained clay for mortar, and with stones built up a little abutment at one end of the forge, to lay his coal and build the fire against. There was no chimney, a hole being left in the roof for the escape of the gas and smoke. He then put a trough at the end of the forge, in which to cool his iron. The floor cost no labor, as it was supplied by mother earth. There was no window, but light came in at the smoke-hole in the roof between the logs and through the chinks of the door, made of joist hewed from small trees, treenailed together and hung on wooden hinges. All this was done little by little, as opportunity offered, and his wife and the children made charcoal by charring wood in the oven, as he could not obtain turf to burn a kiln out of doors in the winter. In mending his chain and staple, Richardson had felt very much the need of something to turn his iron around. One end of a smith's anvil terminates in a point, called the horn, and around which, whenever he wishes to make a hoop, ring, or link of a chain, he can bend it. Richardson had brought into the forest with him a large crowbar. At the expense of much labor with his nail-hammer, he rounded the extremity of the largest end, leaving the rest square; then boring a hole in the stump on the right side, he drove the bar into it. This served as a very good substitute for a horn to his stone anvil, as he could turn a chain link on the round part, and bend iron at right angles on the square edge; and he was not a little proud of it when done.

Richardson's ability to work in wood was well known to his neighbors, but he had carefully concealed his attempts in the blacksmith line, as he did not wish to attract attention till he could obtain tools, and had made some progress. But a matter of such general interest could not long be hid. The children told about their father's mending the chain and the staple, and it was soon known, to the great satisfaction of the neighbors.

This little community, secluded from society and embosomed in the forest, most of them having emigrated from the same neighborhood, and enduring like hardships, were extremely social in their habits, much attached to one another, and ready to make sacrifices for the common good. David Montague was especially beloved by his neighbors, being a man of good abilities, and most open and affectionate disposition. In better circumstances than the rest, he was able to hire help to clear his land, and also kept a horse and a large stock of cattle.

A few days after Richardson had made his preparations, he came in of an evening with his wife, and bringing a chain in his hand, that he flung down at the door. After greetings were exchanged, and they had drawn together around the fire, Montague observed,—

"Neighbor, I hear that you have turned blacksmith, and do your own iron work."

"I'm sure," said Mrs. Montague, "it is going to be a great thing for the place if we have got a smith among us."

"They say," replied Richardson, "that stories never lose anything by going, and I think this is a pretty good proof of it, for it all grew out of this: I went to the village, you know, a while since, to mill, for all hands, and to get some iron work done. While I stood watching Jack Drew, and blowing the bellows for him, I said to myself, 'I could do that work, or I could learn to do it, if I only had his tools and fire, just as well as I can make a pair of wheels, or an axletree, or frame a building, or make a cider-press.' I used to do that kind of work sometimes before I came here. I thought it over going home, and the next time I broke a chain, I set to work with a flat stone before the fire, and mended it, and then I mended a staple; that's the way it came about. I made up my mind then I'd mend my own things, if I could, and save the expense and the long tramp. As we've got only these two rooms, and there isn't much room round the fire, I built a hovel to work in."

"I can tell you, Mr. Montague, he made out firstrate. Husband, show Mr. Montague the chain you mended."

Richardson went to the barn and brought in the chain and the staple.

"Well," said his visitor, after examining the work with great interest, "if you can mend my chain as well as that, I'll never carry another one to Drew, and I'll pay you in cash just what I should have to pay him, and be greatly obliged, besides."

"That's just what I've been telling husband," said his wife; "if he would give his mind to it, get a few tools, and begin in a small way, at first, it would give him work in stormy weather, and times when he couldn't do anything else, be a great accommodation to the neighbors, help the place, and be a good thing all around."

"That's it, Mr. Richardson. Your wife's got the right of it, neighbor. The place is settling, people moving in, and taking up land, stumps rotting, and ground getting fit to plough; and work will grow as fast as you can grow to be able to do it."

"I'll mend your chain, neighbor, in the best fashion I can; but I have to work in such a roundabout way, that I must have my time. Have you got the broken link?"

"No; it flew into the snow, and I couldn't find it."

"Then I shall have to cut one of the links, put the next link in, and weld it."

"I hate to have that done, because it will shorten the chain; and it's barely long enough to bind a load of logs and 'fid' now."

"Haven't you any links lying round?"

"Not I, indeed. Iron is as scarce as money with me, as with all the neighbors. Every link of a chain, piece of a horse or ox shoe, old spike, and every scrap of iron, is worked up. There is one thing, though, I remember now, though I don't know as it's of any use to you."

"What is that?"

"I got Drew to make me a plough-colter, more than a year ago, and found the iron. There was a piece left, a bar about a foot long."

"If I could heat it, and contrive any way to cut it, I could make a link of it."

"I will leave the chain, and send Andrew over with the bar, and if you find that you can't do anything with the bar, why, cut a link and make the chain shorter, for I am determined you shall mend that chain."

Mr. Montague and his wife now took their leave, and in the course of an hour Andrew Montague brought over the bar of iron.

It was the wife's turn to be discouraged now.

"William," she said, "you never can cut that great bar of iron. Why, it's almost as thick as my press-board, and you haven't one single tool to do it with. I'm sorry, but you will certainly have to shorten the chain."

"No, I won't shorten the chain, and I'll find some way to split it and forge a link out of it, if it takes from now till' next spring: that is, if you'll help me. Montague hates to have the chain shortened. It's the first job of work, and I'll do it as he wants it."

"I'll do anything I can; anything in the world, to get bread for the children."

"I'll help you, father; I'm real strong," said Clem, a boy of twelve, afterwards the father of Radcliffe Rich.

"And I, too," said Robert, who was eighteen months younger. Two girls, still younger, would have doubtless volunteered, but they were abed, and not much could reasonably be expected of the baby in the cradle.

William Richardson, in addition to his mechanical ability, was a resolute, powerful man. The encouragement afforded by the visit of Montague, and the prospect of abundance of work, if he could do it, had effectually roused all his energies. His wife, by no means ignorant of her husband's capacities, dismissed her anxieties, for she knew that he would find some way to accomplish whatever he had determined to do.

After sitting a few moments buried in thought, he took a brand from the fire, and his axe, and, followed by Clem, started for the woods, where he soon found a hornbeam tree, the wood of which is very firm and heavy. The boy held the brand while he cut it down, and took off a cut three feet in length. With axe, saw, and auger, by the light of the kitchen fire, he soon made a beetle, that, during the time it lasted,—for he had no iron to hoop it with,— would enable him to strike a harder blow than even a blacksmith's sledge, for it was much heavier, indeed, too heavy for constant use; but a very strong man could swing it for a while, and upon an emergency. He then went down to a brook about an eighth of a mile from the house, for an old axe, kept to save a better one, and to cut ice, in order that the cattle might drink. The axe, by frequent grinding, had become very thick on the edge, and the bitt was rounded.

The next morning Richardson started the fire on his forge with plenty of coal, and put in the bar, while Clem and Rob plied the kitchen bellows by turns, the two little girls looking on with the greatest interest.

To cut iron, less heat is required than to weld it.

"Clem," said Richardson, "call your mother."

The boy returning, said,—

"Mother says one of the girls must come in to watch the cradle."

It was now, "Nan, you go," and "Sue, you go," when the indulgent father, who knew just how the children felt, compromised the matter by bringing the cradle, with the baby sound asleep in it, and setting the sleeper as far as possible from the forge, in order that the noise of the blows might not awaken him.

Richardson, now taking the iron from the fire with the kitchen tongs, placed it on the anvil, and gave it in charge to the boys to hold. He then put the axe-edge down on the iron where he wished to split it, and told his wife how to hold it; then with the beetle he struck heavy blows upon the axe, forcing it into the iron at every stroke, while his wife, after every blow, drew the axe to a new place. The old axe, of excellent temper, and thick edge, that would neither turn nor break, being dipped in water when it became heated, answered the purpose of a chisel admirably, and the beetle was *superb*. Indeed, they would have nearly finished that heat, but the baby waked, screaming, and would not be pacified without his mother. Richardson clapped the iron in the fire, one of the children got a chair, and the mother sitting down, nursed the babe while the iron was heating. After this it became quiet, and the little girls took care of it, while the others cut the iron so nearly through that by bending it back and forth a few times, it fell apart.

He now found that the strip he had cut off was sufficient to make two links by drawing it some. He therefore made two. But it was a deal of work to heat the iron hot enough to weld, because the hand-bellows were single, and only operated by short puffs, the iron cooling in the intervals, whereas a blacksmith's bellows, being double, one part fills while the other is discharging, thus keeping up a steady current of air.

Montague was much pleased when he found that his chain, instead of being made shorter, was lengthened, and now sufficient for all purposes, paid Richardson liberally, and brought another chain that was too short, and had the remainder of his iron put into that.

"There, wife," said Richardson, as he placed the money his neighbor had paid him on the table, "is the first money earned by the hammer. You were just right when you said that mending that staple was the best day's work I ever did, and I'm sure I never earned any money so sweet as this."

CHAPTER III.
EXPERIENCE THE BEST TEACHER.

The morning succeeding the events we have related, David Montague sent over the chain, into which, he wished the rest of his bar of iron worked. Richardson kindled his fire, put in the iron, and began to blow with the hand-bellows; but when he recollected how difficult it was to make iron hot enough to weld in that way, he flung down the little affair, and gave up the undertaking. Convinced that he needed a pair of bellows even more than a hammer or anything else,—for if he could only get a good heat, he could manage to hold the iron with the kitchen tongs, and work it with the claw-hammer,—he resolved to have them, especially as he felt that he could obtain them by his own efforts, without paying out money.

He knew that John Bradford, with whom he was on terms of greater intimacy than any other of his neighbors, had a large lot of logs to haul, and that he was the owner of a whip-saw. Leaving the shop, he went over to John's and said to him,—

"John, I suppose by this time you've heard all about my blacksmithing."

"Reckon I have, and everybody else in this place. They say you hammer the iron on a lapstone, same as a shoemaker his leather."

"Not quite so bad as that; but I find I must have a pair of bellows, and I want inch-and-a-half stuff to make the 'woods.' I have got a pine log at the door, and I can't go eleven miles to a sawmill; indeed, I don't think I could get there with cattle, the snow is so deep. Will you take your saw, and help me saw out the stuff? and I'll take my oxen and haul logs for you."

"Won't I? I'll be right glad to do it."

"Then I'll go home, and get my log on the saw-pit and come over in the morning."

Two men accustomed to the work will saw out boards and plank with a whip-saw as well as they can be sawed in a mill, only it takes more time. Richardson had a place fixed near the bank of the river, where the ground fell off abruptly. Here stringers were laid on uprights set in the ground, on which the log to be sawed was rolled, and the descent of the ground afforded room to work the saw, which is nearly as large as a mill-saw, one man standing on top of the log, and the other on the ground below.

With the aid of his neighbor, Richardson not only sawed out plank enough for the woodwork of his bellows, but one to make a bench, and boards enough to make a door to replace the rude one of poles, and to close a window he meant to make over the bench.

Having procured the material for the woods, the next article needed was leather to cover the woods. Putting on his snow-shoes, he tracked and killed a moose, took the hair off with strong lye, then tanned it with salt and alum, and pounded it upon the anvil with a stick, kneaded it in his hands, and greased it with the marrow of the moose till it was as limp as a rag.

He now made the woods of the bellows, and bows, and as he had neither nails nor tacks, fastened the skin to the woods with wooden pegs. All this he accomplished without much difficulty; but without iron how was he to make the nose, which must enter the fire, or at least must approach within a few inches of it? The nose of a smith's bellows is of iron, and enters what is called the tuyere pipe, which is in these days quite a complicated affair, and communicates with the fire.

"It's no sort of use, William," said his wife; "it must be iron, and you'll have to go to John Drew, and get him to make it."

"I'll sleep a night on it," was the reply, "before I give it up."

Whether he received any information in dreams, or not, I am unable to say; but this much is evident—that he rose in a hopeful frame of mind, and, to the great surprise of his wife, whose whole soul was in the matter, set to work without the least hesitation.

Our readers will recollect that swamps in the forest do not freeze to a great depth, and often, when the snow comes before the cold is severe, not at all. Richardson found clay that he could get at in the swamp, and by cutting the ice obtained sand from the bottom of the brook. He now, with a hoe, broke up all the lumps in the clay, put water to it, and worked it with the hoe till it was fine and tough; then he worked in the sand, made a box a foot square, without ends (by nailing four pieces of boards together), and three feet in length. In the middle of this box he set a pine plug, larger at one end than the other, and tapering to the size he thought requisite, and filled the space between it and the sides of the box with the mixture of clay and sand, ramming it hard with his hammer-handle, in order that there should be no hollow places; put it in the kitchen, where it might dry gradually without freezing; made the frame, and hung his bellows on wooden pins, in default of iron; made the pole to blow with, while a strip of moose-hide served instead of a chain to lift the "wood" of the lower bellows; and then went into the woods to haul logs while his clay was drying, which required time, as the box excluded, in a great measure, the air.

In the mean while, work accumulated on his hands. Reuben Hight brought a chain to be mended, John Bradford a kitchen shovel, the handle of which was broken in two. These shovels were very large, the handle as long as a broom-handle, and the blade nearly as wide as that of a barn shovel. James Potter brought the bail of a Dutch oven; John Skillings wanted a hook made to a chain, and brought a harrow tooth to make it of. Richardson promised to do the whole when he got his bellows done, if he could, of which he felt by no means assured.

The clay was now thoroughly dried, being kept near the fire, and Richardson put the box on the kitchen hearth, and built a very moderate fire. This he gradually increased, till the box was burnt, the plug of pine consumed, and the clay brought to the condition of brick. He then permitted the fire gradually to burn out, and, when the operation was over, he had, as the result, a complete cone, thoroughly burnt. He made a square hole in his butment, put the pipe through it, with the smaller end towards the forge, and bedded it in clay mortar.

Into the large end of this brick cone he put the wooden nose of his bellows. It being a great deal smaller than the cone, he filled around it with clay mortar; his object in giving this shape to the passage being to admit filling, in order to prevent burning the wooden nose of the bellows. The length of the cone prevented its heating sufficiently to burn the bellows-nose by reason of its great distance from the fire, being out of the stone butment, in the cool air; and the clay mortar around the nose was, he thought, a poorer conductor of heat than the brick cone itself.

Richardson completed his work about noon, and it was a good deal of self-denial to him to abstain from making a coal fire at once, and going to work; but he thought it best to let his mortar dry. He, however, satisfied himself that there would be no difficulty in raising all the wind he needed, and he made a small wood fire to dry the clay before it should freeze.

The next morning the shop presented much the appearance of a jubilee. The children had obtained a promise from their father that he would not kindle the fire till they were up. They were out of bed before a ray of light streaked the sky, and the moment breakfast was despatched, the whole family, even to the dog and cat, hastened to the shop. It was Saturday, and Richardson, knowing that Bradford's wife would want to bake, and need the shovel, began with that, putting the two parts in the fire, after having made them ready to weld, or, as he termed it, "shut." He resolved to have a heat this time; put on the coal, and plied the bellows; but by and by he noticed that the iron began to send off sparks, and saw little black specks of charcoal sticking to the iron. Pulling it out of the fire, he found it was all burnt to a honeycomb: that the little black specks of charcoal had burnt into the very substance of the iron, and yet they were black, and the iron came to pieces the moment he struck it. The anvil was covered with scales, and he found it would not weld.

He was sadly puzzled, and most of all, that the charcoal that stuck to the iron, and burnt into it, did not get red hot itself: and he found there was such a thing as getting iron *too hot*. Little Clem had been to John Drew's with his father in the canoe, and now came to the rescue.

"Father," he said, "why don't you do like as Mr. Drew did?"

"How did he do, child?"

"I seed him stick the iron into sand, and once I seed him poke the coal away, and fling the sand right into the fire."

The father now recollected that he had often seen the blacksmith put his iron into sand, but did not know what he did it for. He got some sand, and put the iron into it, then put it into the fire, found the iron did not burn, and he welded it without any more trouble.

He now got along bravely, being able to heat his iron so that it would draw easily. Even the harrow-tooth presented no obstacle; for, after bringing it to a white heat, he got his wife to hold it with the tongs, and using the old axe as a sledge, soon brought the tooth to a size that he could work with his nail-hammer, and finished his job. As to the bellows, they were a great success, afforded a strong blast, and he found the constant current of cold air passing through the cone kept it from becoming hot enough to burn the nose of the bellows.

"William," said his wife, "I'll never say you can't do anything again."

It may seem strange to our readers that Richardson should be able to heat iron sufficiently to be drawn and cut with an axe, and still should have so much difficulty in making it hot enough to weld. They may likewise wish to know what good the sand does.

Iron can be cut and hammered when red hot; but, in order to weld, it must be brought to a white heat—almost melted. When in this state, the two pieces of iron to be united are laid one upon the other, and made to unite by a few smart blows with a hammer. If the operation is rightly performed, the two pieces of iron will become perfectly united, and be as strong at the place where they are welded as elsewhere.

It is, however, quite a nice operation to weld thoroughly. Iron, when highly heated, inclines to oxidize rapidly. This forms a scale similar to that which you perceive on iron when it is rusty. If the two pieces of iron are put together in this condition, these scales that are loose on the iron will prevent the union of the parts. That is the way iron burns up. It oxidizes, and the iron flies off in sparks that are scales red hot. When the smith sees the iron begin to sparkle, he takes it out of the fire, and rolls it in sand, and then puts it in again, or opens the fire, and sprinkles sand upon it. The sand melts, combines with the oxide of iron, and forms silicate of iron, spreads over the surface of the iron, protects it, prevents the formation of scales, and when it is struck with the hammer, leaves the surface clean, and the iron unites perfectly, and forms a solid junction. The smith also leaves the surface of the two pieces to be welded highest in the middle, in order that they may touch there first, and then, when struck with the hammer, the melted sand or oxide will be squeezed out.

The possession of a pair of bellows, with which he was enabled to heat his iron thoroughly, and soften it to such a degree that he could work it with his nail-hammer, proved of the utmost service to our persistent smith, and he was enabled, by the aid of his wife and the children, to mend chains, staples of yokes, domestic utensils, and most of the articles his neighbors brought to him, and, as we have seen in the last chapter, was gaining knowledge even by his mistakes.

But there was a good deal of work that would be more profitable than any he had hitherto done that he was compelled to lose for the want of tools. There were oxen to be shod. Four of the neighbors now kept horses. These they worked before their oxen, and therefore wanted them shod all round, and were obliged to pay John Drew an exorbitant price to leave his shop, and come through the woods on snow-shoes to do it. It was quite as important that he should have iron as tools, in order to learn by practice, as he could not expect his neighbors to find iron for him to spoil in learning. To this end he laid by every cent he earned by his blacksmith work, in order with that, the cloth, butter, and linen yarn, to obtain both.

The tools for the lack of which he was the most crippled in his work were a pair of smiths' tongs, a hammer, and a punch. The kitchen tongs were wretched things to hold iron with. It required all his strength to hold a small piece of iron, and the jaws were so short that it was constantly slipping; whereas, the handles of a smiths' tongs, being crossed like scissor-blades, act as a lever, and the jaws are long, to hold the iron; while a smiths' hammer, being much heavier, and with a larger face, deals a more effective blow, and is, by its form, adapted to the work. In addition to all this, he had but one pair of kitchen tongs, and when he had to weld two pieces of iron, he made a pair of wooden ones, with which his wife took out one of the pieces of iron, and held it till it was "stuck."

He longed—O, how he longed!—for a little iron that he could call his own. It consumed him—this desire—even as does the greed of gold a miser. He reckoned with a piece of charcoal on the top of the bellows the amount of money he had on hand, the cost of getting Drew to make him the tools, and the probable proceeds of the articles he had to sell. To his dismay he found, after purchasing even the few tools he must have, there would remain but a mere trifle with which to buy iron.

"I must," he said to himself, "either go without the iron or the tools. No, I won't; I'll *make* the tools.—I *will* do it, and save the money to buy iron."

Just then his wife came in to call him to supper, and overheard the remark, but did not, as before, say, "William, you never can do it."

CHAPTER IV.
HAMMER AND TONGS.

Most persons accompany the act of close thought with some physical effort; some whittle, smoke, or chew tobacco furiously. William Richardson was not an exception. When he had fed the cattle for night, brought in the night's wood, a turn of water, and renewed the fire, he placed the long handle of his wife's frying-pan across a tub, and began to shell corn.

His wife, who knew there was corn enough shelled for a long time, made no remark, but noticed, while she sat spinning at her flax-wheel, that he dropped a good many ears of corn into the tub half shelled, and some untouched. He was evidently thinking of anything but shelling corn.

Thus they sat an hour or more; not a word spoken. On the other hand, it was whir, whir, whir; scrape, scrape, scrape. At length his wife saw, as the cobs he had been from time to time flinging into the fire caught and blazed, the muscles of his face relax, and a smile flit across it.

"Sue?"

"Well, William."

"Do you think you could get along without the tongs?"

"I do get along without them; they are out to the shop the greater part of the time; I haven't had 'em in my hands, except out there, this three weeks."

"But could you do without 'em altogether?"

"Yes. Why?"

"Because I can make a pair of blacksmith's tongs of 'em."

"Take 'em, husband."

"Could you get along without the fire-shovel?"

"No; because I couldn't clear out the oven."

Whir, whir, whir; scrape, scrape, scrape, for half an hour more.

"Sue!"

"Well."

"Could we get along without one of the andirons?"

"I don't kno-o-w. What in the world can you want of that?"

"To make a hammer."

"We could get along as well without both as without one."

"I don't want the whole of it, only part of the end that's in the fire; we could put a rock under that, and the rest of it would keep the wood from the hearth, and from rolling out."

"Then I would take it, William. We can get along very well, I dare say. Haven't you got corn enough shelled?"

"Haven't you spun long enough?"

"Yes."

"Then we will go to bed."

The sledding was good, and it was sometime before Richardson put his designs into execution. But the sledding broke up, work came in, and he felt the need of the tongs more than ever, as the children were at school, and it was oftentimes impossible for his wife to leave the baby, that was cutting its teeth, and began to be fretful.

He placed a block beside his anvil, knocked the handle out of the old axe, and mortised it into the block, edge up: upon this he could lay hot iron and cut it without calling his wife to assist him.

It was with great reluctance that our smith proceeded to take the tongs and the andiron, when the time came for doing it. "I feel," said he to his wife, "as though I was sheep-stealing: it seems real mean to strip the fireplace, and take your tongs and andirons, especially as we are so miserably off for household stuff."

"I wouldn't feel so, William. The first two years we got along without them; then we thought we needed the tongs, and got John Drew to make them; and now, if you need the hammer more than the tongs, I don't see why you shouldn't take them."

The kitchen tongs were huge affairs; there was more iron in them than in three pairs of light smith's tongs, such as Richardson needed at present, only it was not in the right place, but just the reverse, as the legs of the house tongs were shaped like the human leg and thigh, largest at the fork, and tapering towards the feet, where they terminated in a large, oval lip, very thick and broad, adapted to seize and hold the great brands in the old-fashioned fireplaces; whereas forge-tongs have the most iron in the jaws, and at the cross, and taper from thence to a small size.

To his great delight, Richardson found that he did not need more than half of the legs of the tongs.

"I'll save the body of them," he said, "and when I get some new iron, put on new legs, and Susan can have her tongs again."

He put them into the fire, and cut off the lips, drew down the small end to half its size, in order to save iron, and that the handles might occupy less room in his hand. A new difficulty now presented itself. Indeed, our smith, who was in want of everything but brains and perseverance, trod a brier-planted path. He had no punch to make a hole for the rivet, and without it all his previous work was useless. Punches are made of steel, or, at least, pointed with it; but he had no steel, except his tools and a file, that he needed to sharpen his saws and augers, and could not do without. He knew that an iron punch would answer the purpose; but where should he get the iron to make it of, for he had now discovered that he needed two pairs of tongs, in order to take two pieces of iron from the fire at the same time, to weld, and could spare none from the legs of the fire-tongs for a punch. He took the two oval buttons that had formed the lips of the house-tongs, welded them together, and made his punch. To be sure, at every three or four blows it bent; but he straightened it again, and, by heating the iron as hot as it would bear, succeeded in punching the holes in both pairs of tongs, and then took part of the punch to make the rivets.

So delighted was he when the whole matter was accomplished, that the big man capered around the shop for joy, and ran in to tell the good news to his wife.

"Now, Sue," he said, "let us have a thanksgiving to-day, for I have two pairs of tongs; let us have pea-soup."

There was not much left of the house-tongs, only the head, and about two inches of each leg, below the fork, just enough to weld to. The great benefit of the tongs was instantly apparent. Returning to the shop, William took up what remained of the punch, and exclaiming, "A blacksmith has the advantage of a carpenter, for he can work up his chips," made a hook. This he fastened to a belt around his waist. Of the remainder he made a clasp that he could slip over the handles of the tongs, thus holding the iron and liberating his hand.

Now, if he wanted to use his left hand to hold a punch or cutter, he could put a clasp over the handles of the tongs, and drop them into the hook at his waist; the iron, also, was not slipping out of the tongs and dropping on the ground, every three or four blows. He could now work alone to very good advantage, as he had no large iron to draw, and his wife was not compelled to take her hands out of the dough to help him.

"Wife," said William, when he came in from his work that night, "I am as tired as a dog. It's hard work trying to make something out of nothing." After resting his brain a while, and doing the new work his neighbors had brought, he began to think about making a hammer; so he cut off sufficient iron from one of the andirons, lapped it over, welded it, and formed the body of the tool. But in this a large hole was to be punched to receive a handle. It was necessary that he should have more than one punch, a small one to make the hole, and another to enlarge it, as he could not, with his nail-hammer, strike with sufficient force to drive a large punch through so thick a piece of iron.

"I am sure, wife," he said, "I don't know what I shall get to make punches of. I have a good mind to take one of the teeth out of your flax-comb—they are *steel*—to make the small punch, and cut a piece off the crowbar to make the big one."

"I wouldn't cut the crowbar, William. Take part of the other andiron; we might as well have a stone under the ends of both as under one. There's an old wheel spindle will make the small one."

He acted upon his wife's advice, and made the hammer. Hammers are faced with steel, whereas this was all iron; but Richardson knew that, like his iron punches, it would answer a temporary purpose, and that when it was battered up, he could hammer it back again. He now was able to do all the work his neighbors brought, and in half the time required before. While he was congratulating himself upon his success, David Montague came to the shop, bringing the chain he had mended first; the link had straightened when put to a severe test.

"I know the reason," said Richardson. "I couldn't get a proper heat with the house-bellows." He mended it, and this time there was no failure.

William Richardson, during all these struggles and make-shifts, had learned much, and, in a way that insured its being remembered; had learned the value and use of sand, found that it protected the iron, kept the outside from burning, while the inside was heating; that, if he put two pieces of iron in the fire, and one of them became hot before the other, he could take it out, roll it in sand, and put it back, and the sand would keep it from burning up, while the other was getting ready. He likewise perceived that there was a great difference in the effect of heat upon the different kinds of iron brought to him by his neighbors: some was fine-grained, tough, and would bear a great heat; another kind was coarse, brittle, and, if made too hot, would fly under the hammer, and fall to pieces. Every mistake added to his experience, and he was every day acquiring dexterity in the use of the hammer.

His neighbors, who watched his progress with the greatest interest, were as much delighted as himself, since they were no longer obliged to go through the woods to the village for every little job. They now told him he must learn to shoe oxen and horses, work steel, make axes and plough-irons.

You may well think Richardson was as anxious to be able to do this work as they were to have it done; and the way for the gradual attainment of it came about in the natural order of events.

David Montague had, during the winter, got out the timber for a barn, and employed Richardson to frame, board, and shingle it. This increased his stock of money very sensibly, and he felt that he could now, with the money he had saved by making his tools, the proceeds of his butter, and other matters, and that which he had earned by working for Montague, buy some iron and steel. He had also in the distant future, visions of an iron anvil, that he foresaw he must one day have.

CHAPTER V.
DREW SORE AND SAVAGE.

It was now past the middle of March. A copious rain was succeeded by a sharp frost, making excellent going on the river, and Richardson resolved to improve it; the only drawback being that the river was one glare of ice, and his oxen had lost many of their shoes. He had saved part of the shoes, borrowed some more of John Bradford, and could have put them on himself, as Moody Matthews had a shoeing-hammer, but there were no nails in the neighborhood.

Richardson, however, knew that by taking time and by careful driving, he could get the cattle to the village, and determined to carry the shoes with him, and hire Drew to sharpen and nail them on. He put on the sled half a cord of hemlock bark, his own grist, the butter, cloth, and yarn, together with some corn and grain for his neighbors.

About eight o'clock in the evening his wife went to bed; but William made up a warm fire in the stone fireplace, fed the cattle, and lay down before it. At twelve o'clock he went out, fed the cattle again, and called his wife, who got his breakfast, and he set out. He carried in a basket doughnuts, baked beans, cold boiled pork, Indian bread, and butter, and a jug of coffee, also hay for the oxen. His plan was to stop for the night at Hanson's, who put up teams, paying fifty cents a night for barn-room for the cattle and a bed for himself, Hanson's wife warming his beans, and making tea or coffee for him, as the coffee he carried was to drink on the road. This expense was paid by the neighbors whose errands he did.

At his arrival, he found John Drew, who before had always received him very cordially, in a most surly humor. He was making axes. Tom Breslaw, an apprentice, nearly out of his time, was striking, and blowing the bellows. Barely nodding, in response to the greeting of Richardson, he took an axe, into which he had stuck the steel, from the fire, flung it savagely on the anvil, crying to Tom, "Strike!" and after the heat put it in the fire again, taking not the least notice of Richardson, but giving all his attention to his iron. Finding he was not noticed, and at a loss to know what this strange conduct of the smith meant, he at length said, "Mr. Drew, can you put a few shoes on my oxen?"

"No, I can't. I've got this axe and another one to make for a man that's waitin' for 'em."

"Perhaps you could do it in the morning. I shall be obliged to stay all night to get my grist ground. It would be a great accommodation to me if you could. I had hard work to get the cattle here, and if I am obliged to drive them home as they are, I shall lame them."

"Can't do it, I tell you, and that's the long and short of it."

"Perhaps you could make some nails, lend me a shoeing-hammer, and I would try and nail them on myself. If you don't, I am sure I don't know what I shall do. I had hard work to get the cattle here with no load of any amount. I must haul more back, and I don't know how I can get home."

"And I don't care how you get home, Bill Richardson; nor whether you get home at all. Here I've slaved myself for years, going up to your place through the woods on snow-shoes once or twice every winter, and hauling my tools and shoes on a hand-sled, leaving work here in the shop just to accommodate you folks up there, and took my pay in white beans and all sorts of trash, when I left cash jobs at home and lost 'em; and here you come smelling round, and palavering, as though butter wouldn't melt in your mouth; watch and sneak round, and steal the trade, and then go back, cut off my custom, and take the bread right out of my mouth. Now I've got you where the hair is short. You may shoe your own cattle, you're such a great smith. I won't make you a shoe, nail, lend you a tool, or obleege you in any way, name, or natur'. Strike, Tom Breslaw—what are you gaping at?"

Waiting patiently till the din of blows had subsided, and the iron was returned to the fire, Richardson replied,—

"As for stealing your trade, Mr. Drew, and coming here for the purpose, it is certainly a mistake of yours. I never thought of trying to work a piece of iron till the last time I was here, when the thought came into my mind. You surely can't think it strange, when you know what great labor and expense it is for myself and neighbors to come here, that we should try to do somewhat for ourselves. You would do the same were you in our place. If you complain so bitterly of coming to our place twice a year, what do you think it must be for us to come to you all the time? You must remember, also, that at those times you charged a corresponding price, that was cheerfully paid. I can't well see how you could lose any work by going, as there is no other smith anywhere round, and you must have found the work waiting when you came back. I have never been reputed a thief among my neighbors, or made a practice of stealing. I did wish to obtain some information of you, before I went home, about working and tempering steel, but expected to pay for it. As for taking bread out of your mouth, you have all the work you can do right here, without doing a stroke of work for us."

"Well, all the knowledge you'll worm out of me you may put in your eye, for you won't get any."

"I don't expect, or even desire to, after what has passed between us; but, as I have given you full opportunity to free your mind, and express your opinion of me, any more talk of that kind before my face or behind my back will be at your own risk. I suppose you understand me."

Drew hung his head, and made no reply; for, though a patient and good-natured man, William Richardson was by no means a safe person to provoke.

It was now the dinner hour, and as Richardson left the shop he was followed by Breslaw, who said,—

"Mr. Richardson, where are you going?"

"First, Tom, to your father's, with this bark. He is tanning a couple of hides for me, and told me he would take part of his pay in bark. I was going to buy some iron and steel at the store; but I shall have to give that up; for, as Drew won't shoe my cattle, I shan't be able to haul one pound more than my grist."

"He's a mean wretch, and I don't see how you kept your hands off him. But he's been drinking; that's part of it. Give me your shoes. I'll run into Aunt Sarah's, and get my dinner; it won't take me so long as to go home; and before Drew gets back I'll fit the shoes and make the nails, and this evening we will put them on. Most of the shoes have been on the cattle before. I'll fit the others by them, and if there's any of them too far gone to sharpen, I'll make new ones."

"But where will you get iron? Shan't I run to the store and get some?"

"I keep a little of my own, and do small jobs out of shop time. Any little scraps will do for that."

Richardson hauled his bark to the tan-yard, and Breslaw's father invited him to stop to dinner. As he was passing Drew's shop on his return, Tom came out.

"I've made the shoes and nails, Mr. Richardson; and I'll tell you what I've been thinking of. I suppose money is none too plenty with you."

"You may well say that, Tom; for I'm paying for my land, and every cent counts."

"Well, now, you can, while you are waiting for your grist, go round the village, and pick up old iron, and perhaps some steel, that won't cost you one quarter what it would to buy new at the store, and be just as good, and better, for your use, as it will be smaller, and save hammering. Only look out that it is not too rusty. Perhaps you remember Bosworth, the stone-mason."

"Very well. He made the stones in the grist-mill, and built the piers of the great bridge."

"He died this last winter, and his widow has his drills and other tools, and wants to sell 'em. The drills are all steel, and the best of steel, too; and I've no doubt you could buy 'em for half what the same amount of steel would cost you at the store, and perhaps for even less."

In accordance with this advice, Richardson went to the place, and bought four hand-drills, a foot or more in length, used for splitting stone, and two dozen steel wedges. The latter, he thought, would, at some future time, serve to make toe-calks for horse-shoes. The purchase that delighted him most of all, however, was a churn-drill. This was four feet in length; but only four inches of each end was steel, being much worn, the remainder iron, shaped like the stalk of a seed onion, with a bulb of iron in the middle, three inches in diameter. He also bought a light stone-hammer. This was likewise a great acquisition, as it would serve the purpose of a sledge. Clem could now strike with it for a short time, and would, in a few months, be able to handle it easily; for he was large of his age, and muscular. He could likewise get one of his neighbors to strike, upon an emergency. Pursuing his search, he found several old axes, beetle-rings, three mill-files, the handle of a kitchen shovel, one leg of a pair of kitchen tongs, and an old crane (the latter was a large piece of iron), and some old ox-shoes. At the mill he obtained some of the mill-stone picks that had become too short for use.

Just as he had finished his supper that night, Tom made his appearance at Hanson's with the shoes, nails, and his tools. A rope was procured, and the oxen were cast on the barn floor. Richardson held a candle, stuck into a potato, while Hanson assisted Tom. The latter put on the new shoes, clinched up all the old ones that were loose, and, with a smith's large file, sharpened the dull calks.

He not only refused to take any pay for his work, avowing that Jack Drew was hog enough for one small place, but, sitting down before the fire with Richardson, gave him a great deal of valuable information respecting working iron.

In the morning Richardson rose early, and prepared to start. After paying his expenses at Hanson's, he was able to buy considerable iron at the store, and still had a little money left. The wind was north-west, a bright sun, the ice smooth and hard, and the cattle, sharpshod, were able to travel. Thoroughly rested, and eager to get home, they seemed to regard the load no more than though it had been feathers. Snorting with eagerness, proud of their new shoes, and perhaps elated with the idea of having been to the village, they could at first scarcely be kept from breaking into a run.

Was not Will Richardson a happy man that bright, sunny morning! The keen air braced his limbs, and his heart throbbed with joy. Things had turned out so much better than he anticipated. He feasted his eyes upon the iron and steel—the great bar, the nail rods—he had bought at the store, or rather the thin bar he had purchased to be split into nail rods; for at that day iron did not come from the forges in shapes to suit the smiths, but in large bars, and there was a vast deal of work to be done with the sledge and hammer.

Never did a boy gloat over a ripe plum as did Will Richardson over the great bunch of iron in the middle of that churn-drill. He couldn't keep his eyes off of it, and had already decided in his own mind what use he would make of it.

Thanks to the noble spirit of Tom Breslaw, the cattle travelled so fast that he arrived home long before his wife expected him. The children had come half starved—as children always do in the country—from school, and were screaming, "Do, mother, give me something to eat."

"I'll give you a luncheon, because you'll want to eat with your father when he comes, and you'll want to tie up the cattle, and get the night's wood in, and a turn of water, so you can have time to see him."

This being assented to by Young America, the mother, taking half of a loaf of rye-and-Indian bread, began to spread butter on the loaf, and then cut off and distribute huge slices to the hungry expectants. She had cut off the last slice when the sound of Richardson's voice, shouting to the oxen, came through the half-open door.

"Father—father's come!" screamed the children; and, followed by their mother, they ran to the river. Down the slope they rushed, pell-mell, and, just as the cattle put their fore feet on the edge of the bank, and taking advantage of a momentary pause occasioned by the steepness of the grade, piled on to the sled, the two girls holding on to their father's legs, who, standing on the hinder end of the sled, and holding by one hand to a stake, with the other waved his hat to his wife, shouting, "O, Sue, the best of luck! 'Lashings' of iron and steel; and I've brought back the fulled cloth, and the stuff for your and the children's clothes, and money—only think of it, wife, brought money home with me! You can have your tongs, and your andirons, and I can have all the tools I want? and won't we go ahead?"

His wife was too full to speak; but happiness beamed from every feature, as standing half-leg deep in the snow, she drank in the words of her husband, who, taking her in his arms, seated her upon a bag of meal, and, while the cattle went on, narrated the incidents of his journey, the surliness of Drew, and how nobly it was offset by the generous conduct of Breslaw.

"Ain't it glorious, wife? I tell you what it is, Sue, it's better to be born lucky than rich."

To which we might add, that it is better to be born with brains and energy than rich; for the riches may be lost; but the former are an enduring possession, and when under the control of virtuous principles, a source of unfailing happiness and self-respect.

William Richardson was by no means a talkative man. On the contrary he was by nature reserved and thoughtful. But now his tongue ran like a mill-clapper, and ceased not till the cattle stopped of their own accord before the door.

In the meanwhile his wife remained, listening to the excited narration of her husband, in a sort of silent rapture; but when, after the oxen stopped, he began to show her the iron, and expatiate, saying, "Only see this churn-drill, wife; both ends steel; and what a great bunch of iron in the middle—Swedish iron, too; and three picks, and drills, and wedges—all steel; and that crane—see what a great junk of iron *that* is!—didn't cost me much of anything, either; and that big bar, to make axes; and the thin iron for horse and ox shoes, and nail-rods;"—I say, as he thus ran on, showing and explaining the value of one piece of iron after another, tears of joy ran down the cheeks of the faithful wife, and after that she found her tongue.

Now you needn't laugh, boys, and say, "What a fuss over a little old iron!" It was worth a great deal more to that family than though it had been so much gold; and you needn't say, "O, what a whopper!" Just see if it don't come out so before we have done with the Richardsons. That amount of gold might, and probably would, have ruined them; but on every grain of that rusty metal were written encouragement, inspiration, opportunity; and God Almighty had given to William Richardson the ability to read for himself and his neighbors what was written on those iron leaves.

"Father," cried Clem, seizing the stone-hammer, "what is this awful great hammer for?"

"For you, my son, to help me draw these great bars of iron with—at any rate, by and by, if you can't handle it now."

"I can swing it now, father, just like anything. See here"—swinging it over his head, and bringing it down with considerable force on the iron.

CHAPTER VI.
PATIENT, BUT DETERMINED.

Perhaps our readers would like to know what were the first words Susan Richardson uttered after she found her tongue.

"The first thing I'll do, when I get up to-morrow morning, shall be to spin some linen yarn as fine as I can spin it, scour and bleach it the best I know how, weave it, and if I don't make Tom Breslaw as handsome a pair of linen shirts as any man in this state ever had to his back, it will be because I can't."

The children all had to take a turn at the stone-hammer. Rob could strike with it, but could not swing it over his head; besides being younger, he was much less muscular than Clem, who was very large of his age. Sue could lift it to the height of her shoulders, Sally but a few inches. They now began to carry the iron to the shop. Clem and Rob took each an end of the churn-drill, but the girls insisted on taking hold in the middle, and entirely monopolized the conveyance of the drills, wedges, and smaller things, notwithstanding the boys told them they should think it would look a great deal better for them to go into the house and help their mother get supper. All the satisfaction they got was, "It's nothing to you; mam said we might."

The first work William Richardson did in the shop was with the remnants of the kitchen shovel and tongs he had bought to repair his wife's tongs, and cutting a piece off the old crane, he repaired the andirons.

Sitting on the anvil, he now looked over the iron and steel spread in imposing array by the children over the shop, as a militia captain makes his company take open order on muster-day for the sake of show, reflecting in what way he should make the most of his treasures, when Clem, who had been examining the drills with great interest, striking one upon the other, and listening to the clear, sharp ring thus produced, so different from the dull sound emitted by the iron, said,—

"Father, what is steel?"

The parent, occupied with his reflections, neither heard nor heeded the question.

"Who don't know that, Clem?" replied Robert. "It's what makes father's axe and draw-shave cut: iron won't cut."

"I guess I know that as well as you do. But what makes steel cut any more'n iron? It looks just like it."

"'Cause it's steel."

"You know a great deal about it—don't you?"

"What is it, boys?" said the father, rousing up.

"What is steel, father?"

"It's made out of iron refined and hardened, so as to give it temper."

"What do they do to it?"

"I don't know; it's done in England."

"Will the temper stay there forever?"

"Yes; you can draw it most all out if you heat it, but if you put it in cold water it will come back again."

"What makes you, when you want to burn the handle out of your axe, put wet cloths all over the edge of it?"

"Because I don't want to heat the steel and start the temper."

"What if you did? couldn't you put it into cold water and make it come back?"

"Perhaps I shouldn't get the same temper: if the axe cuts well, I prefer to let well enough alone; if I spoiled it, I should have to go clear to the village to get John Drew to temper it over."

"But, father, I seed you take and put the new broad axe in the fire with no cloth on it, nor nothing, and heat it real hot, so when I spit on it it sissed."

"Yes, my son; but I didn't do that to take the handle out, but to draw the temper. It was so high tempered it broke, and I couldn't do anything with it; so I thought, as it was of no use as it was, I might as well try to draw down the temper, and if I got too much out, it would only be going to Drew after all. Do you understand now, my son?"

"Yes, father; but I heard you tell mother you meant to try to temper an axe."

"I mean to try, dear. That's what I got the iron and steel for."

"Won't you spoil it?"

"I expect I shall, a good many, before I learn."

"Father, I want to see you learn. Can I see you spoil the axes?"

"Yes, child, I shall want you to help me."

"Think you can learn, father?"

"I guess so."

"Then I can learn too. Perhaps there's a man in the steel what lives there and makes it cut."

"If there is, he must have a pretty warm berth sometimes."

"Father, when you learn and I learn, can I make me a hatchet?"

"And me too?" said Robert.

"Yes, I guess so."

Now we intend as briefly as possible to answer Clem's first question. It would be very ridiculous, if a good-looking, nice-feeling boy in the high school, being asked what made his knife cut, should have to stick his thumb in his mouth, look like a dunce, and say, "I don't know."

We must begin with and say a few things in relation to iron, from which steel is made.

The iron ore is put into the furnace, a layer of iron ore and another of coal, together with lime, either in the shape of oyster-shells or stone lime. It is there melted and run into large junks called *pigs*. The lime causes all the flint, sand, and earthy matters to melt and separate from the iron, which, being heaviest, drops to the bottom of the furnace, while the slag, that is lighter; floats on top, and is taken off. This is *cast* iron; you see pigs of it piled up on the wharves in seaports, the outside incrusted with the sand in which it was run, and looking as rough, some of it, as the cinders of a smith's forge. It is highly charged with carbon, coarse, hard, and brittle; can neither be filed, welded, nor worked, under the hammer; is more or less filled with slag and other impurities, and fit only, when melted again and purified, to be cast into pots, pans, stoves, wheels, and various articles. It is now melted two or three times more, and slightly hammered, to beat off some of the slag. Then it is made red hot, and put under steam-hammers. In old times it was hammered by water power, or by men with sledges. This is done in order to take out the carbon, that renders it hard and brittle.

Probably by this time you wish to know what carbon is, to extract which from the iron has cost so much labor. Should I give you the definition of the books, you would probably want that definition defined.

Many boys have seen a diamond: that is carbon in a solid form: pit coal is solid carbon mixed with sulphur, phosphoros, and other elements. Charcoal is solid carbon in a nearly pure state. Carbon has so strong an affinity for oxygen, that when any of the substances that contain it are burned, they give up their carbon, that instantly mingles with the oxygen of the air.

Thus, when iron is heated, its pores are opened, the carbon on the outside is carried away by the air, and more is liberated from within, to pass off in the same way; the object of the frequent meltings and the hammering is to expose new surfaces to contact with the oxygen of the air, and get rid of the carbon, just as the farmer turns his hay, and brings new surfaces to the sun, to dry off the dew.

As the result of this we have wrought iron, soft, tough, of close and fibrous, instead of a crystalline or granular texture, that may be made red hot and quenched in water without hardening or becoming brittle; may be welded, split, punched, made into wheel-tires, hoes, shovels, axes, hammers, pitchforks, knives, or razors. But there is one grand defect in this iron, although it is so tractable that it may be worked under the hammer into a thousand different shapes at the will of the smith; may be drawn into wire so fine as to be woven in a loom or made into a watch spring that weighs only the tenth of a grain, and rolled into leaves as thin as paper, insomuch that a pound of raw iron costing a cent affords steel sufficient for seventy thousand watches, worth one hundred and seventy-five thousand dollars. It is, however, too soft to form a cutting edge that will stand. Make a pitchfork of it, it is harder work to stick it into the hay than it is to pitch the hay, as we know from experience; an axe, it will take all your strength to cut through the bark, and you must grind it every hour; a razor, you can shave but once, and then with tears of agony. Make a hammer of it, and it batters up forthwith; a punch, it bends; a drill, at the first stroke of the sledge it turns.

What next?

Troughs are made of fire-brick, from eight to sixteen feet in length, and two or three feet in depth. The troughs are placed in a furnace, and on the bottom of each of them a mixture of powdered charcoal, ashes, and salt. Bars of wrought iron are laid upon this mixture half an inch apart, to the amount, perhaps, of twelve tons, and covered with charcoal; then another layer of iron and more charcoal, till the trough is full. The top is covered with cement that has been used before, and damp sand. The fire is then made in such a manner that the heat passes all around the troughs, and is kept up from six to ten days, according to the size of the bars and the purposes for which the contents of the troughs are wanted.

The heat of the furnace opens the pores of the iron, and sets free the carbon contained in the charcoal; and as the cement prevents it from escaping and uniting with the oxygen of the air, it enters the pores of the iron and impregnates it. The fire is now suffered to die out, and the metal is taken from the troughs. It is no longer iron, but steel. We now have that which is the "king of metals," and by the aid of which the skilful mechanic can do what would once have been thought miraculous.

The surface of this material is covered with blisters, hence it is called blistered steel. It resounds when struck. Iron once bent remains so; but steel is so elastic that it may be bent to an angle of forty-five degrees, and will spring back to its original position. It is said that Andrew of Ferrara manufactured swords so elastic, that the point of the blade would bend to touch the hilt, and spring back again uninjured. The quality of steel depends upon the quality of the iron from which it is made. The English have carried the art to great perfection, nevertheless are obliged to import the iron from which their razor-steel is made from Sweden. This blistered steel is the kind that lay upon the floor of William Richardson's shop, and in the possession of which he so exulted.

Now you have an article that gives to the axe its temper, the fork its point, the mainspring of the watch its elasticity, and to all tools an enduring edge that may be so attempered as to pierce the hardest rocks and crush the hardest stones; that may be welded to iron, and thus economized. Do you think it strange that Will Richardson rejoiced at the acquisition in his circumstances, or reflected long and seriously in respect to the manner in which he should use his treasures to the best advantage?

And now, perhaps, some thoughtful boy may say,—

"Why be at so great expense of labor and material to take carbon from iron, and then set right at work to put it back again?"

Because there is too much in the cast iron, and so it is all taken out, and just the right amount put in.

"Why not, then, when decarbonizing the cast iron, leave just enough in, and save the labor of three processes?"

This has been attempted, but the results have not given satisfaction. It is not so easy to ascertain when the right amount is left in as when it is put in. The latter can be determined very accurately by means of try-bars, the ends of which are left protruding from the troughs. When, upon drawing one of them out, it is found to be blistered, the process is done. Although blistered steel be so superior to iron, it has imperfections, that impair the quality of edge tools manufactured from it—the result of imperfections in the iron of which it is made. At times there will be differences even in the same bar; one portion will be softer than another, or there will be flaws and shelly places.

When the steel made from such iron is wrought into a tool and ground, the edge is uneven, serrated, softer in one place than another. This amounts to a fatal defect in those articles where great and uniform hardness is required, as in screw-taps, wire-drawers, plates, dies, and stamps for coining and engraving. It is evident, as the carbon is introduced from the surface, that there will be less in the middle than at the outside of the bars; thus the steel is not of a uniform character. In order to obviate this, the bars of steel are made into a fagot heated in a great forge, welded together with a hammer worked by machinery, and drawn into bars, which closes up all the fissures and renders it tough and compact. It is now called shear steel, because shears for dressing cloth were made of it, and it will take a better polish than blistered steel. But the process is not yet completed. Bars of blistered steel that have been the most highly charged with carbon, and are therefore the hardest, are broken into short pieces,—those being put together that are of a like hardness,—and placed in pots of fire-clay, about thirty pounds in a pot, with covers fitting perfectly tight. The pots are placed in a furnace, and the steel in them melted, when it is poured into cast iron moulds, and made into ingots. These are under a tilt-hammer drawn into bars of all sizes. This is cast steel, and it is evident, must be of uniform quality and hardness. This process was discovered in 1750, by a citizen of Sheffield, and for many years kept a secret. It is of this steel that the best tools, swords, knives, and instruments of all kinds are manufactured. But not even shear steel was within the reach of most of the smiths at the date of our story, very little being imported, save in the form of tools.

There is another property pertaining to steel. When heated to a white heat or cherry red, according to its quality, and quenched in water, it becomes hard as glass, and very brittle. The higher the temperature, and the more suddenly it is cooled, the harder and more brittle it becomes. It is this quality that renders steel the "king of metals," and has given to the smith power over all material substances. Even the diamond is forced to yield the palm, for recently steel has been tempered to take its place in cutting glass.

The result of William's reflections was, that, in order to draw and work the large iron now in his possession, he must have better tools and a heavy sledge, as he could upon occasion get one of his neighbors to strike for him. John Bradford lived nearest: he knew that John would be glad to accommodate him, and take his pay in blacksmith work; besides, by employing the same person all the time, that individual would acquire facility, and learn to strike fair.

Commencing with the churn-drill, he cut it off just below the great bulb in the middle, "upset" the end by striking it endwise upon the anvil, and by the aid of Clem, with his stone-hammer, formed it into something like the proper shape for the face end of a sledge. He then partially formed the "pean," or top portion, that in a smith's sledge is wedge-shaped. He wished to punch the hole for the handle before cutting off the rest of the drill, in order to hold it by that part, as he had no tongs that were large enough. To make this hole in so thick a piece needed, he thought, a steel punch, or at least a steel-pointed one. The material was at hand in that part of the drill he had just cut off, only wanting to be pointed.

There was more length than was either necessary or convenient; but he resolved to point first, and shorten it afterwards. Ignorant of the nature of steel, or the degree of heat it will endure, he supposed, as it was very hard, it should be made all the hotter, blew up the fire, and treated it just as he would a piece of wrought iron. The drill had been imported from England,—as were nearly all the tools in that day,—was pointed with the best of double shear steel, and hardened all that it would bear. The result was, that the moment he struck it with his hammer, it crumbled and fell to pieces, like so much brick, till, as there was but about four inches of the steel, nothing remained except the iron to which it had been welded.

Richardson stood looking at the fragments in utter despair. To lose that steel was almost like losing a limb; but it was gone past redemption. It had cost him something to learn that steel will not bear so much heat as iron. Afraid to meddle with the other end of the drill, he resolved, since it needed very little alteration, to take off the corners and square the end on the grindstone; but it proved so hard that he soon gave up the attempt, and felt that he must run the risk.

"I'll try it," he said; "no doubt John Drew spoiled plenty of steel when he was apprentice, and had a master at his back, to boot."

Well aware that the other steel was burned, he watched it narrowly, put on plenty of sand, and before it was white hot, worked it without difficulty.

All he knew in regard to tempering was, that steel becomes hard by being quenched in water while red hot, and if plunged in water after that period, less so; while if suffered to cool of itself, it is not so much harder than iron. He was ignorant of a fact most important to a smith, and by the knowledge of which he is enabled to produce any degree of temper he pleases, after practice and experience of the different qualities of the various kinds of steel; to wit, that the gradations from extreme hardness to extreme softness are denoted by the different colors it assumes while cooling.

Trying with a file the punch that had now cooled on the forge, he found that it was quite soft, and supposed it needed hardening. Heating it as hot as he dared, he plunged it in water, held it there till cold, and then twisted a withe around it for a handle.

He now took a welding heat on his iron, that it might punch the more easily, and set Robert to hold it, while Clem held the punch. So much time was occupied in placing the iron and punch, and instructing the boys how to hold both, that it had cooled, and become harder to punch; nevertheless, he resolved to try it, and lifting the great beetle, struck with all his might upon the punch. At the second blow it broke in two, as short as a pipe-stem.

Clem, who had followed every motion, seeing the blank look of his father, began to cry; while Rob ran to tell his mother.

"Jackass that I was," he said, "to make that punch so hard. Didn't I know that I could punch hot iron with an iron punch, and have done it?"

Finding that there was still a little steel left, he put it in the fire again, let it cool to a black heat before he quenched it, then punched his hole, and finished the sledge. By patient perseverance, and after many ineffectual attempts, he succeeded in learning to weld steel to iron, and made himself several pairs of tongs of different shapes and sizes, also flat punches of files, but of low temper, also chisels. He did not dare to make them hard, as he did the punch; so he let them become almost cold before quenching.

He shod Montague's horse, making all the nails and two new shoes; but he was all day about it, and had nothing better to pare the hoof than a jack-knife. No matter for that—the thing once done, and done right: facility is the result of practice.

CHAPTER VII.
HE FINDS THE CLUE.

Thus far our smith had by no means realized the benefits anticipated from the possession of steel. He had, indeed, ascertained what degree of heat it would bear, learned to weld it to iron, made some punches that were a little better than iron ones, and yet he was as far removed from a knowledge of tempering that would enable him to forge and finish a reliable tool of any kind as before; since to heat a piece of steel and plunge it in water, making it so hard and brittle as to be useless, or quenching it when nearly cold, thus rendering it about as soft as iron, did not amount to anything practically.

And yet this man aspired to make an axe; yes, even had dim visions of plane-irons, draw-shaves, chisels, and gouges manufactured by William Richardson, edge tool maker. Aspired, did I say? The expression is too feeble. The idea absorbed his thoughts, and, ever present to his mind, assumed the character of a passion. It was not a mere whim, but based upon solid grounds.

There were but few ploughs in the place, and not many horses, and they were not shod all round except in the winter. But the axe was in universal use, subject to continual wear, and frequently broken. John Drew was celebrated for giving to his axes a high temper, that rendered them liable to break in frosty weather; one cause of which probably was, that he made up a lot of axes, and then tempered the lot. Upon tempering days he was always more or less under the influence of liquor. Indeed, he thought he could not temper an axe properly, unless he was half drunk; and it must be allowed that many of his neighbors were of the same opinion, while others said, he wanted them to break, in order that he might have a job of repairing. It was too early in the season to plough; the ice had broken up in the river, and having first driven the logs, cut and hauled in the winter, to the mill, he gave his undivided attention to the work, and employed John Bradford to help him cut up and draw the large bar of iron purchased at the store, while Clem and Robert mounted on a block—not being tall enough to reach the handle without— and blew the bellows. John had not struck through two heats with the large sledge when the stone anvil broke in two. This mishap, however, was soon repaired, as there was no lack of stones.

While they were placing another stone on the stump, David Montague came in.

"Neighbor Richardson," said he, "it is too bad that a man who is possessed of the industry and ingenuity you are, should be so put to it for tools, and be obliged to work iron on a stone. Now I tell you what I'll do with you. I mean to get out timber and boards in the course of next year to build me a frame house the year after; 'twill take two years to make the shingles and clapboards, hew the frame, and put the house up. Now I'll advance you money to buy an anvil beck (beak) horn, stake, tools to head nails with, and you may pay me in work, shoe my horse and oxen, and make all the nails for my house. I shan't want a nail under a year, and not many under fourteen months, so that you can make them next winter, and at odd jobs."

Nails were then made by hand, of wrought iron. The stake was a species of anvil of small size, and used to point horse-nails on. The beak horn was a very necessary thing at that day, used for welding hollow articles, and for work upon plough irons.

"I am sure, neighbor, you couldn't do me a greater favor, for I need an anvil sadly, though I can get along without the stake and the beck horn."

"You can, perhaps, at present, but you will soon need them both. I don't think you ought to feel under the least obligation to me, for in advancing this money, I am benefiting myself and the whole neighborhood more than you. It will save me and all of us many a hard tramp through the woods. Besides, I don't like to get down on my knees to John Drew, beg him to work for me, and then pay him twice as much as it is worth."

"So I say, neighbor," said Bradford, "though—to give the devil his due— Drew is as good a blacksmith as ever stood behind an anvil, but mighty uncomfortable. But where are you going to get the bricks, neighbor, to build your chimneys?"

"Make them, John; there's sand and clay both in my pasture. So you see there's work enough for two years to hew the frame, make the shingles and clapboards, cut logs for boards, and make and burn the bricks."

Richardson improved the opportunity, while assisted by Bradford, to forge the polls or iron portion of two axes, and split up iron for nail-rods and also for horseshoes. He had never seen any one temper a tool, but he had often struck for Drew to forge axes; had seen him weld the steel to the iron, and knew he could do that. Although he had hired John to help him draw the large iron, because he could not do it, even with the aid of the boys, without great outlay of both time and labor, he didn't care to expose his awkwardness before him. In short, he preferred to be alone while adventuring upon this portion of the work, in order that he might study out the matter as he went along with no witness to his mistake but the boys, and as for tempering, we have seen how little he knew in respect to that.

The next morning he made his steel in the shape of a wedge, and split a corresponding crevice in the blade of the axe, and not quite so wide as the steel was thick, in order that it might bind on the sides as it entered, to hold it while heating, and put the whole in the fire for a weld. At the first trial the steel fell out on the ground the moment he struck it, and he lost his heat. He now shut the slit together so that the steel did not quite reach to the bottom, closed it up on the steel a little harder, put the axe in the fire, and before striking, struck the edge of the steel against the side of the anvil, to drive it home to the bottom of the slit, and thus succeeded in making a perfect weld.

But now came the crisis—to temper it. All depended upon this. So important a tool was an axe at that day, men wouldn't hesitate to travel twenty miles additional to a smith who had the reputation of excelling in the art, and no excellence of form or finish could compensate an axe-man for its absence.

He was well aware the reason the punch broke was on account of its hardness, and also that if he had, after putting it in water, let it cool some, it would have been less brittle; but he also knew the harder a tool is, the keener it cuts, and, forgetful of the fault in Drew's axes, imagined he could not get it too hard to cut wood. He thought there must be a vast difference between wood and iron, and that the harder the better; it would never break in wood.

Therefore, after finishing as well as he could, he made it as hot as he could without burning, and quenched it, put in a handle, and set to work grinding. The axe proved so hard, although he had made the blade very thin by hammering, that it was almost impossible to grind it, though he put a liberal allowance of sand on the stone. Susan and the boys took turns at the stone, the father encouraging them by declaring that it would cut like a ribbon, for it was harder than Pharaoh's heart.

The implement was ground at length. Richardson whet the edge and forthwith proceeded to a large hemlock that grew near, to try it. If unskilled in making, he was very far from being a novice in the use of an axe.

At the first blow he cried to his family, who were all gathered at the foot of the tree, his wife with the babe in her arms,—

"It's going to cut; I know it is."

Leaving the keen instrument buried in the wood, he pulled off his outer garments. The blows now fell thick and heavy.

"Cuts like a razor. Throws the chips well. Never saw an axe work easier in the wood," broke from him at intervals, while the children clapped their hands and capered around the tree till it came crashing to the ground.

The hemlock was scrubby, and one of the lower limbs was dead. Richardson struck the axe into it with all his might; but when he pulled it out, there was a piece of steel out of the middle of the bitt as large as a half-dollar.

Greatly to the surprise of his wife, he manifested no symptoms of discouragement at this disappointment in the moment of victory; he merely said, as with one foot on the butt of the tree, he looked at the shining and crystalline surface of the fracture,—

"Well, I've found out the temper that will shave the wood. I must now find out the highest temper that will stand hemlock knots."

The next thing Richardson did was to try with a file his saw and a draw-shave that cut well. He found they bore no comparison in hardness with the axe he had just broken, yet they were both wood tools, and good ones. He then tried a chopping axe made by Drew. It was softer still, but it cut well and stood hemlock, fir, and spruce knots. He now understood that tools for wood, especially where blows were given, did not admit of a very high temper.

"I wish," he said, "I did know how it is that blacksmiths tell when steel cools down to a right temper. How I wish I had asked Tom Breslaw!" He sat down on the butt of the tree to reflect. Clem seated himself by his side, while Robert, standing on the tree, wiped the drops of sweat from his father's brow.

"Father," said Clem, at length, clambering into his parent's lap, "what you going to do with the axe now?"

"I'm going," said he, putting his arm fondly around the little questioner, "to try and make it just hard enough to cut, and not break or turn."

"How will you know, father, when you've got just enough out?"

"Guess at it. I can't do any better. If I only had a watch or clock, I'd let it cool two minutes, then four, and see what that would do. Do you understand, my little man?"

"I don't know, father; ain't it just like when mother takes a candle, makes a mark on it with her knitting needle, and says, 'When the candle burns down to that mark, 'twill be half an hour, and then you'll have to go to bed, Clem?'"

"Something like it; but I want something that will tell the minutes."

"Then it would be two minutes hard, father," cried Clem, who, with both arms around his parent's neck, had almost got into his mouth. "How funny! Shall I go borrow Mr. Montague's watch?"

"Not now, dear."

Taking the boy by the hand, and the axe in the other hand, he walked thoughtfully towards the shop.

After heating to a cherry red, he laid it on the forge to cool, began to count, and continued counting till the axe was cool. He then chalked down the number on his bellows.

"Father?"

"Don't bother me now, dear;" and he began to think aloud.

"This axe was as hard as glass before I het it; now the temper's all out. It has taken while I could count sixty-four to come out. Now, if sixty-four takes out the whole, thirty-two ought to take out half, sixteen a quarter, eight an eighth. The temper is put into steel when it's put into water; and the hotter the steel, and the quicker the chill, the harder it is. What made that axe so hard was, that I het it so hot, and chilled it quick. If I had made it only half as hot, and then put it in water, the temper wouldn't have begun but half as soon, and then it would have been only half as hard. I guess that axe's about an eighth too hard. I'll heat it just as hot as I did before, and count eight, then put it in water. I wonder if that'll be the same thing as though I hardened it at full heat, and after that found some rule by which to reduce the temper. I'm afraid it won't. Let me think of it." He sat down on the forge, while Clem, not daring to speak, stood with his great round eyes staring anxiously in his father's face.

"I had an axe of John Drew once that was too hard—kept breaking; but it cut like a razor. I was afraid to touch it to draw the temper; but one day I put the 'poll' of it in the fire to burn the handle out, and the wet cloths I had on the steel to keep it cool got dry while I was talking with a neighbor, and the poll got red hot. I thought I'd drawn all the temper out and spoilt it, but after that it was just hard enough. Now I'll just do the same thing again."

He heated the whole axe, steel, and all, then quenched the whole of the steel in water till it was cold, leaving the rest of the axe red hot.

"Now I'll let that hot iron draw on the steel while I count eight."

He did thus, then quenched the whole; tried it in the knot; it broke, but very little; put it in again, and counted sixteen. It was too soft; the edge turned.

"I don't believe but that red-hot iron draws too savage on the steel; takes the temper out too fast. I'll draw it more gradual and count the same number of times."

He now dipped the whole axe in water, edge first, took it out directly, put the poll only on the outside of the fire to keep up a gradual heat, counted sixteen and quenched it. The axe cut much better and neither broke nor turned. He thought he would heat it, count but twelve, and thus see if it wouldn't bear a little higher temper. Just as he was about to take it from the fire little Sue came to call him to dinner.

"Tell your mother I can't come yet; don't know when I can come; to eat dinner, and not wait for me."

"Nor me, nuther," said Clem. "I ain't coming till father comes."

He quenched the axe, put the poll on the fire, and while looking at it and counting, thought he noticed a flaw in the steel. Rubbing it in the sand and coal-dust of the forge till it was bright, he found it was only the edge of a scale raised by the frequent heats. But his attention was instantly arrested by seeing the bright steel change under his eye to a pale yellow, commencing at the point where the steel joined the iron, and gradually extending over it; while he looked, it changed to a darker shade, became brown, almost purple. He had now counted twelve, and quenched it. When he took the axe from the water, the same tinge was on the steel. The axe now cut better and stood well. But he had got hold of an idea he meant to follow out.

"I wonder what those colors are," he said. "Who knows but they may be the temper? Just as fast as the temper was let down they changed—grew darker. Wonder what they would have come to, if I hadn't quenched the steel. I'll know." Heating the axe once more, he rubbed it bright, and looked for the colors. For a little time the steel was white; then the pale straw color appeared again, growing darker, till it became brown, with purple spots, then purple, light blue, pigeon blue; then darker, almost black.

"O, father, what handsome colors!"

No reply. Much excited, he quenched the steel, and determined to ascertain whether the colors represented different degrees of hardness. When he found, by careful experiment, they did, he caught the wondering boy in his arms, ran into the house crying,—

"Now, my boy, we've got something that's a better regulator than David Montague's watch, your mother's candle, or counting, either."

Entering the house he shouted,—

"Sue, I've got it! I've found how the blacksmith's do it, or, if I haven't, I've found a way just as good."

His progress was now rapid; he soon ascertained the proper temper for all kinds of tools. The steel of the axe he had experimented with had been through the fire so many times that the life of it was all gone. He therefore put new steel in it, improved the shape somewhat, ground the whole surface of it before tempering, to take off the hammer marks,—for he had not learned to hammer smooth,—tempered it carefully, and hid it away in the shop.

The next week he procured his anvil, beak-horn, stake, and tools for nails. They came from Boston to Portsmouth, from thence to Kennebunkport, by water; on an ox team to the village, and from there up the river in a canoe.

His land joined Bradford's, and they had appointed a day to build a piece of log fence together. Richardson took his new axe with him, having ground it sharp. Watching his opportunity while Bradford was putting some top poles on the fence, he took Bradford's axe, putting his own in the same place. Bradford, without noticing the difference, took it up and began to chop into the side of a tree.

"Whew! How this axe cuts! Gnaws right into the wood. It ain't my axe; it's William's. Will, where'd you get this axe?"

"Made it."

"The dogs you did."

"It is one of those you helped me forge."

"It's worth two of that axe you are using that John Drew made me. Will you sell it?"

"Yes; that's what I made it for."

"May I put it into the knots?"

"Yes; try it in any fair way, and if it breaks or turns, you needn't take it."

Bradford, after making a thorough trial, took it. It was soon noised round that William Richardson had made an axe for John Bradford that beat Drew's all hollow. Every body wondered at the ease with which he took up anything, little knowing the struggle it cost him.

His farming work now came on; but at intervals he made axes that found a ready sale. He made a small pair of bellows in the fall, and a little forge in the chimney corner. The boys learned to make nails, and made nearly all Montague's nails in the winter evenings. He paid less and less attention to farming, and more to working in iron, paid for his land, and built him a frame house. In the autumn of the year that he made the first axe, he found that he could not well make ox and horse-shoes without a vice, and resolved to make something that would answer the purpose.

He began by taking two wide, flat bars of iron, and turned the edge of them over the edge of the anvil, like the head of a railroad spike, in order that, when the flat surfaces came together, these edges might make a face to the vice. To the other ends of each of the bars he welded pieces of the old crane, rendering that portion of the vice that was to fasten to the bench long enough to reach to the ground, and rise eight inches above the edge of the bench, and welded an old horse-shoe on the back side to fasten it to the bench. The other he made but two-thirds as long, and by making a slot in one, with a hole for a pin, and punching an eye in the other, he contrived both to connect them, and form a hinge joint on which the outer leg of the vice might traverse. Two holes were now punched to receive a bolt that was designed to answer the purpose of a screw, one end of which terminated in a head; the remaining portion was punched at short distances with eyes very long and wide, to receive broad, thick keys or wedges that would endure hard driving.

He now set up the permanent portion of his vice, put the lower end into a flat rock set in the ground, and fastened the upper part to the bench, brought up the other side, and put the bolt through both. The hinge at the bottom permitted the outer jaw of the vice to play back and forth on the bolt in order to open or close it. By means of tapering wedges driven into the eyes in the bolt, he could wedge a piece of iron firmly into his vice to file it, could turn the calks of a horse-shoe or set them at any angle he wished. Whenever the vice did not come up to the eye, and the wedge would not draw, he slipped washers—iron rings—over the bolt to fill the space, and then entering the point of his key, drove it with great force. It was not very convenient, but it answered the purpose effectually, for it was substituting the power of the wedge for that of the screw.

"Mother," said Clem, one morning, "will you let me have a piece of your tongs?"

"My tongs, child? What do you want of my tongs?"

"To make some bow-pins—iron ones—for my steer's yoke; father's gone, and said we might play."

"No, child; you're crazy."

"You let father have 'em."

"Well, that was because he wanted a pair of tongs to hold his iron."

"So I want the bow-pins."

"Well, I shan't have my tongs spoilt for nonsense."

"Mother, is that red and white rooster mine?"

"Yes."

"Mine to do what I'm a mind to with?"

"Yes."

In the course of half an hour, Clem, with his rooster under his arm, presented himself at David Montague's door.

"Good morning, Clem. What are you going to do with that rooster?"

"I want to sell him. Andrew said you wanted one."

"Yes; mine froze last winter. What do you ask for him?"

"I'll sell him for that horse-shoe what's hanging on your barn-yard fence."

"What on earth do you want of that horse-shoe?"

"I want to make some bow-pins for my steers."

"Well, you may have it, and after you have made 'em, I want to see 'em."

As William Richardson came home, he saw smoke coming out of the chimney of the shop, and heard the sound of the hammer and sledge. Looking through a chink, he saw the boys busy enough. Clem was behind the anvil. They had flattened out the heel calks of the horse-shoe, straightened it, and lapped one part over the other. Just as he looked in, Clem was putting sand on it; in a few moments he took it from the fire, welding hot: Robert struck with the sledge, and they soon drew it out into a thin, square bar.

"I hope you ain't wasting my iron, boys."

"No, father," said Clem, "it's mine. I sold my rooster to Mr. Montague, and bought it. We are going to make some bow-pins, and we don't want anybody to help nor show us; we want to do it."

At this hint Richardson walked into the house. When Clem took the bow-pins to Mr. Montague, the latter told him to make two pairs, and he would buy them of him.

Settlers now began to flock in; a carriage road was made through the woods; wagons and carts came into use. Montague and others built a sawmill and a grist-mill; the town was incorporated, and Richardson made the mill-chain. This was a wonderful advance from mending the ox-chain before the kitchen fire on a flat stone.

"Neighbor Richardson," said Montague, as he came to get his horse shod, "I was coming home from the village last Tuesday, and met Sam Parker going to get screw-bolts made. Now, it always galls me to have work go out of this place. I think you'd better send to Boston and get tools, so that you can cut screws whenever they are wanted; there will be more call for them every day, for the town is growing fast."

"Thank you, neighbor. I'll think of it."

He resolved to see if he could not make something that would cut screws, before sending to Boston.

It is said that the idea of the principle of gravitation was suggested to Sir Isaac Newton by seeing an apple fall from a tree. He wondered what made it drop to the earth, rather than go in the opposite direction. However that may be, it is certain that a thoughtful man will receive suggestions from things that make no impress upon the stupid and careless.

As William Richardson sat before the fire that night reflecting upon the conversation with Montague, he noticed Clem putting powder into a horn. The boy had rolled a leaf of his last year's writing-book into the form of a tunnel, fastened it with a pin, and was pouring the powder through it.

When the boy had finished, he said,—

"Clem, hand me that paper before you unpin it."

After looking attentively at it for some time, he said to the boy, who, interested in whatever attracted his father's attention, was looking over his shoulder,—

"Clem, the lines on that paper are a screw."

"Be they, father?"

"Unpin the paper."

Clem did so, and they were all straight again.

"How funny, father!"

"Get my square, and you, Robert, go to the wood-pile and get a piece of birch bark—white birch."

After stripping the bark to a thin sheet, he cut it square. He then set off an inch at one corner, and drew a line from that mark to the corner of the paper on the same side, making an oblique line.

"You see that is up hill, boys—don't you?"

"Yes, father."

He then wrapped the bark round the broom-handle.

"Now it climbs right up the broom-handle; that's the way a screw does; it's just getting up hill by going round."

"What's the good of it, father?" said Clem, who was altogether of a practical turn, but had never seen a screw.

"I'm going to try to make one in the morning; then you'll see."

The next day he made a steel bolt, or blank, tapering, and of the size of the screws he thought would be generally needed, leaving the head square, and sufficient length of steel to hold it by in the vice. The next thing to determine was, the pitch or inclination of the thread, and its size. On the edge of a piece of birch bark he set off quarter of an inch, and drew a line from that mark to the edge of the bark, and cut it off, giving the rise or pitch. It was the time of year when boys make whistles. He cut an elder sprout just the size of his bolt, spit on it, and pounded it on his knee with the handle of his knife till the bark came off; this bark he slipped over the bolt, pounded up and boiled some pieces of moose horns, made glue and glued it on solid, put the strip of birch bark around the lower part of the bolt, its straight edge in line with the lower edge, and glued it on. There was now a perfectly true spiral round the bolt, the quarter of an inch offset determining the inclination, and also the size of the thread. He now filed out a fork from a thin piece of iron just a quarter of an inch in width, the two points, chisel-edged, one sixteenth of an inch in width each, leaving a space of two sixteenths between them. Commencing at the narrow end of the birch bark, he followed along its edge, cutting the bark sheath as he went, till he came again to the point from which he started, having cut two spirals through to the steel, with a ridge of bark between them two sixteenths of an inch wide. Putting one side of his fork in the furrow already made, he followed round till he came to the head of the bolt. Placing it in the vice with a three-cornered file, he cut out his thread, the ridges of bark on each side forming a guide for a true thread. With file and cold-chisel he cut out segments in the middle of his bolt, the whole length, leaving the thread on the corners unbroken, thus forming a cutting edge at each corner where the thread was broken. He now hardened and tempered it.

As the next stage of the process, he forged a steel plate,—the ends terminating in handles,—in which he made round holes of various sizes, corresponding to the size of the two ends of his bolt. Into these holes he put this hardened steel screw-tap with plenty of bear's grease, turning it forcibly round with a wrench till the sharp edges at the squares cut a thread on the inside of the hole, and then hardened the plate. With this plate he could cut a screw on the head of a bolt, and with the screw could cut a thread on the inside of a nut. Seizing his broadaxe, he hewed a great spot on one of the logs of the shop, and wrote on it with chalk,—

Having paid for his land, and being able to buy iron, and in the possession of suitable tools to work with, he resolved to make a proper vice with a screw, instead of a bolt. He made the vice-body, taking pattern from John Drew's, of English make; but the screw of a vice must be square threaded, not a diamond thread, like those he had hitherto made; since, being in constant use, the thread would wear off in a short time. He laid out the screw in the same manner as before, except that instead of sheathing it in bark, he dipped it in beeswax till it was coated, and cut the thread with a file and cold-chisel, and instead of putting the screw through both parts of the vice, made a box for it to work in. It is evident he could not cut a thread in the box, that must be square, like that of the screw, with a screw that was square-threaded; neither could he do it with a chisel or file. He did it in this way: he hammered out some steel wire large enough to more than fill the thread of the screw, and wound it around it; then he drove the screw with the wire on it hard into the box, filling it completely, and fastened the ends of the wire. He then turned the screw carefully back, and took it out, leaving the hole lined with the wire.

Richardson had in the house a brass plate that had been on a soldier's belt, and procured from Montague the brass top of a fire-shovel; these he cut up and filed up, putting the filings and pieces into the box between the coils of wire with borax. He wrapped the whole box in clay mortar, and dried the mass; then put it in the fire till the clay was red hot, and the brass melted, which soldered the coils of wire fast to the sides of the box, forming a thread.

With the two springs of a broken fox-trap welded together, he made a spring to throw back the jaw of his vice when the screw was turned. After accomplishing all this, he built a frame shop with a brick chimney, paying Montague in work for the bricks, laying them himself; and now he considered himself entitled to wear a leather apron.

CHAPTER VIII.
A TRADE THE BEST INHERITANCE.

The boys standing, as it were, upon their father's shoulders, sympathizing with and aiding him to the utmost of their ability, early obtained a knowledge of working iron far beyond their years, and contracted a love for the occupation, especially Clem, who seemed to inherit all the patience, energy and originality of his father, together with an amiable disposition and strength of limb. Until Clem was nineteen they lived at home, doing nearly all the farming work, and at the same time helping their father in the shop. They were then desirous of going where a better quality of work was demanded than in their native place.

"Well, boys," said Richardson, "I'm entirely willing you should go. I began too late—had too little to do with, no tools, and poverty to struggle with—to accomplish much. I've done the best I could; but I want you to have a better chance. I think you've both got the mechanical principle in you, and had better go where you can work it out, have tools to work with, and learn all that comes up."

They went to Portsmouth, New Hampshire, where their father had relatives, and after working a week on trial, were both hired as journeymen. Clem never wanted to meddle with anything but edge tools, displaying remarkable ability for that kind of work, while Robert proved an excellent shoer, and had but few equals in wheel-tiring and all kinds of carriage work. He could also make a wheel as well as iron it, and manifested his father's ability for working in wood. Learning the use of hammer and file when mere children, and growing up to it, their work had a finish about it that is seldom attained by those who commence work in manhood, and when their habits are formed.

After perfecting their trade, they hired a shop and set up business for themselves, Clem devoting the greater part of his time to making edge tools, while Robert attended to the other portion of the work. Business was good, and they accumulated property, and frequently sent money to their parents, and cherished a strong affection for their native place, going home every year to Thanksgiving.

When the boys had been a year from home, their father went to visit them. At his leaving, the boys would have loaded him with tools,—"swages," "fullers," "screw-taps," "drills," and "shears," to cut iron,—but he refused to take them.

"You know, boys," said he, "I like to make things myself, and think as much again of anything I make myself. I'm just as much obliged to you as though I took them. I've seen all the tools you have here, and been round among the shops and seen all the ways they do their work, and I'll go home and make every one of these tools; and I think I can improve upon some of them. I've got help now, for Henry Bradford, John's boy, is coming to work with me, and learn the trade—that is, learn what little I know."

Finding he did not incline to take the tools, they put a lot of iron and steel on board the sloop in which he started to return by the way of Kennebunk, or, rather, Cape Porpoise, which was the landing-place then.

There was a little girl, Lucy Armstrong, who went to school with Clem when it was kept in David Montague's house, and they formed a childhood liking for each other which continued and strengthened as they grew older. Lucy was a girl of excellent abilities, the best scholar in the school, and as she grew up manifested qualities that are not often united. She possessed great energy of character, a robust constitution, and most affectionate disposition. Everybody loved and pitied Lucy; for her girlhood was embittered by many trials and sorrows.

Her father she never saw to recognize; he was killed by a bear when she was a babe, and her mother was taken away when she was four years old. Lucy, after her mother's death, went to live with an uncle—her father's brother. He was a hard, penurious man, and his wife resembled him, being a morose, griping woman, with no children of her own to draw out her affections and sweeten her disposition. She made poor Lucy serve with rigor. She was poorly clad, poorly fed, went barefoot in the summer and till late in the fall, was obliged to work both out doors and in. When dropping corn and potatoes in the spring, her feet were red as a pigeon's with cold, and in the fall they bled from being pricked with the stubble. In the cold nights of November she must sit in the barn and husk corn. The old folks did not intend to be cruel; but they had been hardly dealt by themselves in childhood and youth, and hard treatment renders people hard and callous in their treatment of others.

In one respect they faithfully discharged their duty—in sending her to school every day so long as it kept, which was at first but six weeks in the winter, but by the time Lucy was thirteen increased to fourteen weeks; and after the town was incorporated and the ordinances of the gospel established, she went to meeting every Sabbath. School days and Sundays were the green spots, and all the green spots, in Lucy's cheerless life of incessant toil, save the few moments when sent to hunt eggs; and hidden in the haymow from the eagle eye of her aunt, she read Clem's letters for the hundredth time. Clem seldom came to the house; a visit from him put her aunt into a perfect fury, as she was unwilling to lose so good a drudge.

"Get married!" she would say, "yes, that's all girls nowadays think of. Wonder what they expect to live on. Better get something ahead first."

Although how she was to get anything ahead while spending her youth and strength in their service did not appear, especially as her uncle had made his will, and left all his property to a nephew as close-fisted as himself. He often remarked "that he meant to leave what he had got by hard knocks to somebody who knew how to take kere of it."

"Clem," said Robert, when the time during which they had hired as journeymen had nearly expired, "if ever you mean to marry that girl, why don't you do it? What do you let her stay there for, suffer everything but death, slave herself, and dry up, working for that old skinflint and his woman? They'd move into a mustard seed, and then have rooms to let. If you don't, I'll go and court her myself."

"I mean to the moment I feel that I can support her comfortably. You know I'm like father—one of the kind to cut my garment according to the cloth. I don't want to make her worse off than she is now."

"That's impossible. Get along with you; go hire two rooms somewhere, and then go and get her. I'll board with you. Nothing comes amiss to her; she's a treasure of a girl, smart as steel, and pleasant as a May morning. What did father and mother have when they set up, and see where they are now."

Clem took his brother's advice. Lucy's aunt raved like a mad woman at first; but when she found that it was no use, and the neighbors were all against her, she calmed down, gave Lucy a bed and pillows stuffed with turkey feathers, and said they would be on the town before two years. She proved a false prophetess. In two years they were blessed with a nice baby. Clem and Robert had all the work they could do, the hammer going every evening till nine o'clock in the winter months, though they still lived in two rooms, with the privilege of another for occasional use. They continued to thrive till the war of 1812, when the brothers took a contract from the government to bore cannon, which, proving a very profitable job, left them with abundant means. Robert still continued to board with his brother, and, remaining single, put all his money into the firm.

William Richardson, accumulating property by his trade, bought a piece of timber land every year, and let it lie. In the latter part of his life the rise in the value of this land made him affluent. At his decease this portion of his property fell to the sons, his wife having died some years before him, and the daughters receiving their portion in money. The shop remained as it was; Clem would have nothing touched. It was not, to be sure, the original log hovel; but it was the same forge, and the building stood on the same spot. The old pine stump still formed the anvil block, and the hammer fashioned from the andirons still lay on the anvil, just as his father had left it after his last day's work. There also were the tongs made from the legs of the kitchen tongs, and the sledge forged from the churn-drill.

After the war business revived, and there was a great demand for lumber. The Richardsons sold out at Portsmouth, returned to their native place, bought the old mill privilege, and went to lumbering. Strange to say, Clement Richardson and his wife, although retaining their simple and industrious habits, felt that they did not want their children to work as hard as they had; and going to the other extreme, while affording them all the advantages of education and culture their altered circumstances enabled them to bestow, trained them up in a way that rendered them in all matters of practical life absolutely helpless.

This, as our readers know, was the character of Rich when he entered college; he could scarcely tie his own shoes. The good fortune of stumbling upon Morton for a while roused the energies that lay buried beneath this effeminate training; but after separating from his mates, he relapsed gradually into his former habits.

Thus passed the first year after leaving college; but with the succeeding spring came something that, like to the shock of an earthquake, effectually roused Rich from his poetic reveries and visions of high art, rent with a rude hand the tissue of the dream-robe fancy had woven, and set him face to face with the bitter, stern realities of life.

Clement Richardson was naturally a prudent man, averse to incurring risk of any kind; but uninterrupted success in all his plans for thirteen years had rendered him sanguine. He found, soon after engaging in lumbering, that very little was to be realized from small operations; that, to accumulate, a person must either possess the capital and risk it, or hire money and run the risk of losing that. He and his brother, stimulated by the high price of lumber at that time, and intoxicated by good fortune in lesser adventures, hired money largely, and expended every dollar of their own in land and logs. They had a good drive, early in the spring the logs were in the booms, and the mills running night and day to manufacture them, in order to meet demands that were fast maturing. The price of lumber was still high, future prospects were most flattering, and the Richardsons felt that a fortune was within their grasp, when rain began to fall while the water was still almost at freshet pitch, and there was much snow in the woods at the head waters of the river.

Clement concealed his anxiety from his children, and in some measure from his wife, who, although she knew that great loss would follow the breaking of the booms, was utterly ignorant of the extent of her husband's liabilities and of the crisis at hand.

Directly after supper the two brothers went out. Rich occupied a good portion of the evening in reciting to his mother and sisters a poem he had spent weeks in composing. After the children had retired, Lucy Richardson sat sewing, wondering at the continued absence of her husband and his brother, and listening to the roar of water. At length there came a crash; she with difficulty suppressed a scream. In a few moments a servant came to tell her one of the mills had gone.

"Where is my husband, Henry?"

"He and Mr. Robert are watching the boom."

Another weary hour passed, when Clement Richardson came in; he was pale, haggard, and dripping with water.

"Lucy," he said, "I am *ruined* and *Robert* with me. All the money we had outside of our real estate was in those logs, and they have gone into the Atlantic, the mills with them, and it will take all our real estate, furniture, and the house over our heads to pay the money we've borrowed." In those days creditors made a clean sweep, took everything worth taking, and the wife's property was held for the husband's debts.

"It's a great misfortune, husband; but it might have been much worse."

"Worse, Lucy? How can a man lose more than all?"

"It would have been worse to lose health,—worse to lose our love for each other, if such a thing could be,—worse to have a wicked, disobedient, or deformed child; and I am sure it would be worse to lose character, which you won't if you have property enough left to pay all you owe. It would certainly have been worse had it come when we were past labor; and I'm sure we were happier before we moved into this house, and when you were working at your trade, than we have ever been since."

"But the children, Lucy. I see it all now as one sees everything when it is too late. We thought we had enough for them and us, and have taught them everything except how to take care of themselves."

"They will learn that. They are not too old to learn."

The property of the brothers, very valuable, was sold, and the proceeds divided among the creditors, who all relinquished voluntarily the interest on their demands. This left the brothers, after paying everything, one hundred and fifty dollars, as the remnant of a large property. David Montague was dead; but his son Andrew inherited not only his father's property, but his principles. One of the creditors, he bid off the old Richardson homestead, house, shop, and outbuildings. As soon as the business was settled, he offered Clement Richardson money to go into business again. The latter thanked him for the offer, but said he intended, as soon as he could find a place to work, to go back to his anvil.

"Clem," said Andrew Montague, "our fathers come here and cut the first trees together, and lived and died fast friends; you and I have grown up together, and been just as good friends. I know you are proud-spirited, and I love you all the better for it; but I beg of you, let me do this much. There is the old shop; nothing has been disturbed; and there are the tools your father *began* with, and those more modern ones he used in his latter days. Take it, rent free, and I'll bring you a fortnight's work to-morrow morning. I will let you have the house as soon as Coleman, whose family are sick, leaves it."

"I'll take it, Andrew, in the spirit in which it is offered, and may God bless you. There's luck in that old hammer that lies on the anvil where father left it. The first blow I ever struck on iron I struck with that, and the first work I ever did was to make a pair of bow-pins for your father."

As soon as Morton could leave the scholars he was instructing in private, he set forward in the stage to see Rich, and well aware, by letters received, of what had occurred, made inquiries, on arriving, for the shop. Peering into the door around the corner of another building, he saw a tall, strong-built man, past middle age, fitting a horse-shoe at the anvil. Another person, of about the same age, but more slightly built, was tearing the shoe from a horse's foot. A bar of iron was heating in the fire, apparently to make a new shoe, and at the bellows stood Rich, the glory of Radcliffe, class poet, elegant scholar; those finely-cut and delicate features, that no one could look upon without interest, begrimed with smut, save where partially streaked with streams of sweat; for it was a warm afternoon in May. As he turned towards the fire, to look at the iron, Morton slipped behind him and laid his hand upon the shoulders of Rich.

CHAPTER IX.
BLOOD WILL TELL.

The mingled expression of heart-felt delight, surprise, and consternation that pervaded the features of Rich, when, upon turning, he looked Morton in the face, was quite ludicrous.

"Mort!" he gasped.

"Yes, Mort," replied his visitor, grasping fervently the hand that was timidly extended to meet his own; "ain't you glad to see me?"

"Glad!" shouted Rich, grasping both the hands of Morton in his own, while the tears ran down his cheeks; "I hope you don't think I am not; but—"

"But you are in a working dress, and not in a state to receive me, who never cleaned out the president's barn, milked his cow, or dug his potatoes, and you are smutty."

Thus saying, Morton rubbed his hand on the top of the bellows, and made an awful smut spot across the whole side of his face.

"Will that remove your scruples, old chum? How are you?"

"O, Mort, I'm so glad to see you!"

"Expected you'd be; that's what I came for; didn't come for anything else; 'kalkerlated,' as Uncle Tim would say, to make you glad."

Rich now introduced Morton to his father and uncle, who received him without any of the embarrassment that had overwhelmed Rich, and in a most hearty manner.

"You must excuse, Mr. Morton," said Clement, "my son's constraint upon first seeing you; it was occasioned by the recollection of the change in our circumstances, in consequence of which he cannot entertain as he would wish the friend he loves so dearly, and whom we have all learned through him to love, even before meeting. If we have been unfortunate, it is no more than has overtaken more deserving persons than ourselves, and our losses have neither chilled our hearts nor discouraged us from effort."

"We think," said Robert, "that as we earned all we have lost by our own industry, we can, by the same means, better our condition."

"I am sorry, Mr. Morton," said Clement, "to be obliged to keep my son till this horse is shod, as the owner is waiting, and there is a new shoe to make; but after that he will be at liberty.—Strike, Robert."

Rich, eager to be released, struck with good will; the sparks flew all over the shop, and a second heat put the iron in such shape that Mr. Richardson required no further help. Rich flung off his leather apron, washed himself in a bucket, and wiped the smut from Mort's cheek with a towel that did not put on much more dirt than it took off, when they left to cleanse themselves more effectually at the house.

The dwelling was old, out of repair, and consisted of three rooms on the ground floor, but two of them plastered, and a low attic. If Morton felt depressed by finding his friends in such wretched quarters, he could not but admire and wonder at the energy and cheerfulness with which Rich, his father, mother, and uncle bore up under their reverses. The girls, however, appeared chagrined and depressed, and seemed to him completely heart-broken. They were considerably older than Rich, some children having died between them. Rich, and Morton, after supper went to walk, the former observing that by reason of their limited accommodations there was no opportunity for conversation in the house. Following a footpath that led along the bank of the river, they entered a noble orchard, just commencing to blossom. It lay upon a declivity sloping to the river. Passing through it, they came to a swale sprinkled with elms, and commanding a fine view of the river, and flung themselves on the grass side by side.

"Rich," said Morton, "do you know what has surprised me more than anything else I have met with here?"

"I should think the pickle you found me in when you came into the shop."

"No; it is to find yourself and your parents in such good spirits. Most men, after having met with so great and sudden a reverse, would have become entirely disheartened, and I expected to find *you* completely prostrated."

"The cheerfulness is not assumed for the occasion, Mort."

"I know that, you could not deceive me in such a matter."

"Believe me, as far as I am concerned, and were it not for my sisters, and seeing my parents compelled to renew in their old age the hardships of their youth, I should be happier to-day than for the last year and a half, for I have now a clear conscience."

"What have you done? What crime have you committed to set your conscience in arms?"

"The crime of doing nothing; of wasting myself. You know what fine speeches I used to make in college about effort, setting the standard high, and all that sort of thing, and how pat at my tongue's end I always had '*per angusta ad augusta'* (I'm in a way to realize one part of it now, I think); and as long as I was neck and neck with you and Hill, I did do somewhat; but after I came home, I just fell right back into the old ruts; could not make up my mind in regard to a profession; didn't really want to. I was too comfortable; but I felt mean, felt guilty. When I went to Portland, and heard you argue that case, and saw how much labor it had cost you, and how nobly you came out of it, I felt meaner still, and was half inclined to return without seeing you, and resolved when I got home I would go to work; but I took it out in thinking so, till the trouble came like a flash of lightning; since then, I trust, I've done something, and been of some little use."

"Was it, then, so sudden? I knew that your father's difficulties came in consequence of his lumber and mills being carried away; but even a freshet gives some warning."

"None of us knew that father had every dollar invested in logs that were like to go down stream. He and uncle were anxious enough, but kept it to themselves; and the very night it came, when every man about the mills was out in the pouring rain watching for trouble, I was fooling—reciting a poem that I was going to deliver to a company of our young folks; and I'm ashamed to say, that what I am now going to tell you I had from Henry Alden, one of the men who was where I ought to have been, with my father at the time. You see that smooth, perpendicular ledge that makes out into the river?"

"Yes,"

"And that stake driven into a crack in the ledge?"

"Yes."

"When the water is up to that stake it is freshet pitch. All the morning and afternoon the water had been rising; in the evening, it was the same till it reached a fearful height, when one of the mills went. My father and Uncle Robert stood under that ledge with a lantern, watching the marks they had made on it with chalk. The rain had stopped, and for the last hour the water had not risen, the clouds had broken away overhead, and the stars came out. Every one of the men (all old river-drivers) thought the danger was over. 'Robert,' said my father, 'I think the booms will hold; the rain is over, and the river will soon fall.' The words were scarcely out of his mouth before there was a great cry from the bank above that the logs were coming. Henry said father turned pale, but never opened his mouth, or turned to look, but went straight home. When I came to the breakfast table the next morning, father was sitting there, a little paler than usual, but just as calm as ever, and told us what had taken place. You see now how sudden it must have been to me, mother, and the girls, and almost as much so to him, for he thought the crisis had passed."

"Why didn't the boom break before? and how came it to break after the water was done rising?"

"About two miles above this place is a large intervale, where a great quantity of hay is cut. Upon this flat stood a large barn, with no cattle in it, used for storing hay; half a mile below this was a toll-bridge. The water undermined the barn, and started it from its foundations, and down it came against the bridge with an awful crash. The toll-house stood on piles outside of the bridge. It struck the bridge within ten feet of the house, in which the toll-keeper, his wife, and three children, one a babe in arms, were sound asleep, they supposing, as did my father, that the danger was over. Awakened by the shock, and thinking, in their fright, the house was going, they ran out on to the bridge, the mother with the babe in her arms, all in their night clothes, and were swept off, with about twenty-five feet of the bridge. If they had staid in the house they would have been all right, for there it remained on its own foundation. The barn, bridge, a parcel of fences and drift stuff, all came down into our upper boom together, broke that and then the lower one. One mill had gone before. This vast mass, borne on the raging torrent, carried away another, half the grist mill, and a carding mill."

THE BREAKING OF THE BOOM. Page 119.

"What became of the family on the bridge?"

"The barn, being so big, and taking so much wind, went ahead of the bridge, that was low in the water, and when they got down where the river was narrower, some men went off in a canoe and took them ashore."

"Rich, I am going to hazard a supposition. Will you tell me if I am correct in it?"

"I'll tell you anything I know."

"You belong to a strong, resolute breed of men. Any person looking at your father as he stands at the anvil, and your uncle, can see where you came from. It is not in accordance with the make-up of persons having such blood in their veins to live without effort or object. It causes them to despise themselves—the meanest of all feelings, because the rugged nature craves hardship. When you exerted yourself to the utmost in college studies, chopped wood and hewed timber, although there was no necessity for it; when in that tremendous race at Brunswick, through gullies, thorns, coal kilns, dogs, and mires, you gave me, who had the advantage of years of training, all I could do, and distanced all the rest, that was the true nature asserting itself. I can understand why it was that, after crossing the Alps, settling down in Capua, and becoming effeminate, you lost your own self-respect, and were unhappy, and also how these feelings were all intensified when you found that while ruin was impending, your father's mind racked with agony, you were writing verses to school girls, wasting time and talents, and throwing away opportunities that would never come again. I can understand, likewise, why, when you took your portion of the load and felt that your father was encouraged by your aid and sympathy, you regained self-respect, and experienced relief and comparative happiness. But there is much more I cannot fathom."

"What is that, Mort?"

"Well, there is a light in your eye, and an expression of quiet, trustful happiness in your face, that were never there before, and that are not to be accounted for by anything you have yet told me, or that I have observed here. It seems to me that while summoning all your own resources to meet this exigency, you have gone out of yourself for aid; and that, to my mind, accounts perfectly for all the results, and renders happiness in untoward circumstances no mystery."

"Mort, I am going to answer your question, but not directly, because I don't feel quite sure of myself yet. When we were in college there was perfect sympathy between us. Perk, Hill, Savage, and the rest, had their ups and downs, fallings out and makings up; but between you and me there was never a shadow or a chill. We were as completely one in sentiment and affection as that mist that's rising over the river; but after you went to hear Mr. Sewall, and wrote me about it, there seemed to be a dark shadow between us. I couldn't tell what it was, and I didn't love you any the less, but somehow there was a difference. Mort, since this trouble came I've read your letters over, and understand them as I never did before. That shadow is gone, and the sun shines all over."

"I know what you mean, Rich; you need say no more."

"Now, Mort, this orchard, the swale, and all this land to the river, were part of our place. You have seen where we live now, and I suppose you would like to see the spot we left; if so, we had better go before it gets dark."

"Perhaps you don't care to go."

"Yes, I do. I don't dislike to go. Father might have put it into somebody's hands to cheat his creditors, and still lived there, as many have done; but he paid his debts with that and other property, and went behind the anvil; and every time I go there I consider what a temptation he resisted, and feel proud of him. I don't know how others may feel, neither do I care; but I had much rather have for my father a poor man of principle, than a wealthy rascal; blood-blisters on every finger, and earn my bread by hard blows on hot iron, than to feel the very clothes I wore, and the luxuries I enjoyed, were swift witnesses against me."

It was plain enough to Morton that the grindstone grit of poverty was fast cutting away the iron that overlaid the steel, and bringing out the true temper. So delighted was he, that he could not forbear shaking Rich. A playful scuffle followed, in which Morton by no means attained the usual advantage.

"I tell you what it is, Mort," said Rich, "let me work at the anvil and you study law a while longer, and I'll lay you on your back, and mud both shoulders."

"It is always a pleasure to me to see a young man ambitious, for even if he places his standard beyond the measure of his capacity, he is likely to make the most of himself. I've got something in view when I go back that will offset your sledge-hammer. See if I don't make your backbone crack the next time we take hold, old fellow."

"I should like to know what kind of exercise it is. I'm sure you can't hew timber there."

"A churn-drill, my boy. What do you think of that? Ain't that a good deal like work? Won't there be some misery to that? There's a man by the name of Noble, who blows rocks on Oak Street. He has two churn-drills. I am going to use one of them as soon as he gets it steeled."

"You please yourself with that idea, young man, will you? You can't start a hole with a churn-drill as it ought to be. I can tell you, it takes a workman to do that. Your drill will bind, and you'll get stuck."

"I know I can't at first, but he'll start the holes for me and then I can churn; and after a while I shall learn to start my own holes, and strike true."

"You'll get sick of it. It is the hardest work that is done."

"Did you ever know me to get sick of, or give up anything, I undertook?"

"Yes, I have."

"Name it, slanderer, name it. Don't think to escape by dealing in generalities. I demand date and place. When and where did I get sick of anything, and give it up?"

"On the twenty-fifth of December, Christmas night, quarter before seven, you got sick of eating pork pie at Uncle Tim Longley's, and Granny Longley gave you a dose of thoroughwort tea, and made you *give it up*."

"If we are going to see that house, it is time we were about it, for it is almost sundown, and will soon be dark."

CHAPTER X.
DEAD LOW WATER.

They ascended the rising ground, passing along the edge of the orchard, till, upon gaining the height of land, they entered upon a broad, level field of twenty-five acres, smooth as a lawn, green in all the verdure of spring, and giving promise of an abundant yield of grass. A variety of forest trees were scattered over it, among which the walnut and white oak predominated. Here and there a clover head was seen, and bobolinks, balancing on spears of herd's grass, were exhibiting themselves to the best advantage, while now and then a forward apple tree on the warmer ground was covered with white and red blossoms.

"Your father never planted these trees," said Morton, gazing at the massive trunks, covered with moss and rough scaly bark; "who did?"

"I'm sure I don't know whether it was the wind, the crows, bears, or squirrels, but they were here when the white men came."

In the centre of the field stood the mansion house. It was painted white, with green blinds, and, seen through the mass of foliage by which the house was surrounded, the color produced a very pleasing effect, being scarcely more prominent than the streak of white peeping through the green folds of an opening rose-bud.

Several very large white birches were scattered in front of the buildings among other trees, that beautiful green peculiar to the leaves of this tree in the spring contrasting pleasantly with the white bark of the trunk and branches. The house, fronting the river, stood endwise to the main road, from which a broad avenue led to it, approaching by a gradual curve the front, a less spacious one conducting to the back portion and the out-buildings. Both of these avenues were lined with the Lombardy poplar, then highly prized throughout New England as an ornamental tree. They still linger, a few in nearly every town, often rising with decaying branches over some grass-grown cellar—sole memento of a departed generation.

The mansion, standing in the midst of this vast green, large on the ground, and high studded, without a fence to belittle the effect and obstruct the view, with abundant out-buildings, well arranged and in perfect repair, as seen through the mass of foliage, produced an impression better felt than described.

Morton, enraptured with the sight, stood long before the main entrance silent, his arm in that of his friend. At length his eyes moistened as he said,—

"Rich, I never saw anything like this spot; so grand and beautiful! Everything is fresh, in perfect repair, and yet these oaks and birches seem two hundred years old. I never saw such trees, except in the forest. I shouldn't be in the least surprised to see a black bear acorning in one of them."

"I've no doubt they have done it. I've heard my grandfather say that the whole of this land between us and the river was a heavy growth of such trees as you see here, except the low ground, where it was yellow birch, white maple, and elm; that a man by the name of Dingley, who was well off, came here from Salem, built this house, cleared the land, all but about two acres in front of the house; but his wife died, and his two boys didn't want to stay here—wanted to go to sea. He went back to Salem just before the embargo, and let the place to the halves. Then a friend of his—another Salem captain, who had made money going to the coast of Africa, when the embargo put a stop to his business—bought it. He also spent money at a great rate; made the house almost over, built stables, took away the fences, and as he was determined to have just what trees he wanted, and didn't mind expense, selected those he wished to remain, cut down the rest, and all the underbrush, and hauled the trunks and brush off, because he knew, if he put fire into it, he should kill the whole. That's the way, grandfather said, these old trees came to be left here.

"While Captain Norris was building, planting, clearing, and turning everything upside down, and making improvements, after some models he had seen abroad, and while the embargo and the war of 1812 lasted, he was contented; but when he had made about all the improvements his purse would allow, and maritime business began to revive after the war, he was as uneasy as a fish out of water, and sold the place to my father, with all his improvements, for half what it had cost him, and went back to Salem, and to sea again."

"It must have been a sad day to you, when you came to take leave of this home, and—"

"And go to the place where you found us, you mean. Well, it was a bitter day to all of us, but there were some reasons that made it especially so to me. Father and mother had known sorrow, and so had my sisters. I had a little brother and sister, neither of whom I ever saw. They died within a year of each other, and my sisters were old enough to realize it. But never since I can remember has there been a cloud in our sky till now. Father was prosperous, I was petted and indulged, had all I wanted, loved my books and my parents (never knew how much I did love them till now), and never had a sorrow, except when some pet animal died; but those tears were soon dried, and when I awoke the next morning the sorrow was all forgotten in some new pleasure, or some new pet. It seems to me now that I was just like one of the humming-birds that always come to the honeysuckle that hangs over that western window.—By the way, that was my room, Mort."

"I see it all, Rich; and now, let me tell you, I wasn't in a very cheerful frame when, on my way to college, I met you at Portland. I had left home, and was looking forward to a four years' course at college, with hardly any funds, and the prospect for the future was gloomy enough, when you came across my path, just like a gleam of sunshine, and appeared so buoyant, happy, and trustful, that I said to myself, 'There's a boy that's grown up in some happy home, without a care or sorrow.'"

"Just so, Mort. But there was another thing which gave to this place a charm for me that it did not possess for the rest of our family."

"What was that?"

"I'll tell you. The girls were born in Portsmouth, and their earliest associations were there. My father and mother also have had homes at other spots; but if I was not born here, I grew up among these great trees, and, I can tell you, the very roots of them were in my heart, and it was hard parting. One of the very first things I can remember is, crawling out of the front door, when mother's attention was turned, and making for dear life towards that birch with the hang-bird's nest on it. Sometimes in my haste, I'd tumble down the steps—roll from the top to the bottom. If it half killed me, I wouldn't cry, for fear mother would come and get me before I reached the tree; and when she did, O, didn't I yell some? Here I made my little gardens, dug wells, and put water in 'em; here I had my pets, hens and ducks, pigeons, and kittens, and birds; and when any of them died, I buried them under that walnut with the drooping branches, because I thought it felt sorry for me. I didn't have many playmates, for I was a shy boy, and so I loved the trees, birds, and flowers all the more, and played with them, and my sisters, and Uncle Robert. You see that large maple that stands next to the hemlock— the biggest tree in the field?"

"Yes, it is almost as large as the great pine in the glen at Brunswick."

"Don't you think, when I was a little thing, wore long clothes, red stockings, and red morocco shoes, my father tapped that tree, and used to give us the sap to drink. One washing day, when they were all busy, I got away, ran for the maple, and got down on my hands and knees to drink out of the trough. I was having the nicest time, putting down the sap, when a bee came whiz in my face, struck me on my upper lip, and ran his stinger in the whole length. I suppose he thought I was going to drink up all the sap, and he shouldn't get any. The girl was hanging out clothes, heard an outcry, and saw me flat on my back, kicking and screaming. She ran, and mother ran, and my sisters, and such a time as there was when mother pulled the stinger out. I tell you, Mort, no other place ever seems like the one where you played when you were little."

"That's so, Rich. The corn in the dish on the table don't taste half so good as that you roast out doors, and down with it, all over smut and ashes, and half raw; and the apples they carry round in the evening at home don't begin with the ones you've hid in the haymow, and eat when they are so full of frost it makes your teeth ache."

"We might have staid in the house through the summer. It is empty, and like to be; but father and mother said they had rather go at once than be dreading it. The neighbors were very kind, and helped us move (what little we had to move), as everything of any value went to the creditors, with the exception of my books and stock of tools; that father didn't give up, because he said they were my tools, with which to earn my bread. They had been given to me by him when he was solvent, and the creditors could not touch them.

"During the labor and excitement of moving, and before the neighbors, we strove to appear as cheerful as possible; but when all was over, and we came out on to this platform where we are sitting, each bearing something that had been forgotten,—I my violin and a pair of andirons, mother her press-board and a coffee-pot, the girls knives, forks, and spoons, father shovel and tongs,—I tell you, the sound of the bolt going into its place when he locked the door gave me a heartache.

"After we got off the steps, and turned round to take a last look at the old home, that never seemed half so lovely before, we couldn't any of us keep the tears back. I don't know but you will think it weak, but it made me feel real bad to see my dog, Fowler, wagging his tail, and frisking as though it was a holiday, and I almost wished I was a dog."

"Weak, Rich? A boy that could leave a home like that, where all his associations were formed, as he would leave an inn, or get out of a stage-coach, and never look back, could not be a friend of mine."

"The old cat would not go. She came and rubbed up against my legs, then went back, sat on the steps, looked after us, and mewed when we called her, but would not come.

"'Give me your things, my son,' said father, 'and go and get her.'

"I took her up, and carried her with us, but she went back the next day."

"I see a black and white cat now," said Morton, "sitting on the spur root of yonder big white oak."

Rich called, "Puss, Puss." The cat came running, jumped into his lap, and put her fore paws on the collar of his vest, opening and shutting her claws, lifting her feet up, and putting them down in the same place, as cats do when they feel happy, rubbing the side of her face against his chin, and shoving her nose between his vest and shirt bosom, and purring all the time.

"She loves me," said Rich, "but she can't bear to leave the old place.—We must go, Mort. Our folks won't know what has become of us. I do wish you could have come up here to thanksgiving, as you were going to do when we were in college, and the place was ours. To see it now is very much like looking at persons after they are dead—the house all shut up, and nothing alive but a homesick, heart-broken cat."

CHAPTER XI.
A STRIKING CONTRAST.

They walked along some time, each busied with the reflections excited by the previous conversation.

"Mort," said Rich at length, "I'm sorry, but you'll have to sleep in a poor place to-night."

"We've slept together in David Johnson's barn, in Peleg Curtis's fish-house, on a pile of wet menhaden nets, and in the woods on Great French. Didn't we make a fire and warm the ledge on the north-west side of Hope Island, sweep off the coals, and lie down—in November too?"

"Yes; but when folks go to visit their friends, they expect a little better treatment than when camping out. Don't you remember when we used to walk down to Maquoit of an afternoon in June, just before anything had faded, and it was high water, how beautiful everything looked? the sharp line of color, where the points fringed with the bright green of the thatch parted the blue water, the bolder outlines of the gray rocks, and the trees reflected in the calm water; and yet go down there two or three days after, at low tide, and there would be only a hundred acres of steaming flats, the shores and the grass on their edge strown with kelp, dead clams, horse-shoe crabs, dead limbs of trees, dead fish, chips, and rotten eel grass; no water to be seen nearer than a mile and a half!"

"Indeed I do; and the contrast was so great that one must be possessed of a most devout spirit not to arraign the order of nature, and wish it was high water all the time."

"I'm sure I can't imagine what should put Maquoit Bay in my head to-night, unless it was meeting with you, and thinking of old times; but it seems to set forth my condition exactly. Six weeks ago it was high water with us, a spring tide, up over everything, clear to the grass ground, filling every cove and creek, the mouths of the brooks kissing the birch roots on the edge of the cliffs, and lifting up the strawberry leaves. Now it is dead low water, bare flats, angry sky, and to me the voyage of life seems 'bound in shallows and in miseries.'"

"That's one side, old chum" (putting his arms around Rich's neck), "but the tide only ebbs to flow again. The farther it runs off, and the more it drains out at one time, the higher it flows the next."

It was the first manifestation of anything like depression that Morton had noticed in his friend. Rich, however, shook it off, as the bird shakes the dew from its plumage, saying, with a smile,—

"You are right, Mort; and that's the way I look at it generally; but I can't yet visit the old home, and come away again, without stirring up something that had better be kept down; especially when the cat puts her head in my bosom, as she did to-night, and says, 'Do stay here with me, I am so lonesome.'"

Morton, as they came in sight of the house now occupied by the Richardsons, was most forcibly struck with the contrast between this abode and the one they had just left. Their present habitation stood in a tan-yard; indeed it had, in the days of his poverty, been the residence of the owner of the tan-yard, who being pinched for room, had crowded his house into the smallest possible limits.

It was placed very near the line of the street, leaving barely space for a single doorstep, which was a pasture stone. The tan-pits at one side approached within two feet of the cellar wall. On the other was a currier's shop, leaving just space enough between the two buildings for a narrow cart road. Beneath the back windows of this shop were old oil barrels and heaps of curriers' shavings, stewing and simmering in the sun.

Directly behind the house a garden spot twenty-five feet by thirty was fenced out. It had not been ploughed for some years; the Richardsons did not care to cultivate it, as their stay was but temporary, and it was overgrown with weeds, and strewn with old boots and shoes, broken pottery, pots and pans that had outlived their usefulness, heaps of ashes, and the bleaching bones of cats that had come to an untimely end.

Abutting on this lot was a large shed, open on the side facing the dwelling in which was the "beam" house, where the green and bloody hides were received and "fleshed." Here were heaps of horns, and the pith or marrow that comes out of them when they taint. The roof of this shed was covered with glue skins, that is, the trimmings of the hides saved to make glue, spread to dry, and which attracted swarms of green flies; add to this a stagnant mill pond that supplied water for the pits, and to propel a bark mill, fences, and walls hung with sides of leather spread out to dry, and smeared, or, in technical language, dubbed, with tallow and rancid fish oil, and you have a faithful description of the surroundings of this delightful abode. But aside from actual experience, imagination cannot conceive or tongue describe the combined odors furnished by these various substances when operated upon by sun and wind.

The house was in perfect keeping with the site upon which it stood. The walls were covered with shingles, two courses of which had rotted away near the foundations, in consequence of banking up the walls with earth; part of the top of the chimney had fallen off, and lay on the roof that in places was bare of shingles and covered with moss.

Upon entering the house, a door on the left opened into the kitchen, the plastering of which was the color of milk and molasses, and appeared to have been flung on, and then clawed in by cats, affording in the furrows lodgments for smoke and secure harbors of refuge for flies. At the back of this room was a small bedroom, finished in the same manner, with the exception of being sealed to the height of a chair, and the wood work painted with a color intended, probably, for red; it, however, looked very much as though a hog had been killed on it. In this apartment the parents slept. Another door, on the right, admitted to an unfinished room, with a rough floor. Here were Rich's lathe and tool chest, a pair of cart wheels finished, except smoothing up, and a wheelbarrow that only required ironing.

"This is my workshop," said Rich. "My mechanical genius, that used to expend itself on flower-pots and vases, in turning canes and cups, tops and nine-pins, balls and drum-sticks, is now directed by stern necessity, into a more useful channel; and, believe me, when I have made a pair of wheels, got my money for them, and bought provisions for the family, I feel a great deal better satisfied with myself than I used to after spending two or three days making something that was a mere plaything, or at best only served the purpose of ornament."

At each end of the garret was a window, and there two bedrooms were made, with rough board partitions, one of which was occupied by the two daughters, the other by Rich. Here was his library, that was quite extensive, his father having indulged his fondness for books, among which was a German edition of the classics.

The room was small, and the roof of a low pitch. The book-cases, writing-desk, bureau, and chairs all occupied so much of the room that the bedstead was necessarily pushed far under the eaves in order to afford space enough in the middle to move around and stand upright.

"It is quite convenient," said Rich, as they entered, "for you can reach everything without getting out of your chair."

"And then to consider," replied Morton, in the same vein, "that the most celebrated philosophers and poets have meditated and sung in garrets."

"True," said Rich; "but I suspect it would be far more pleasant to meditate about than it will to occupy it come next dog days. Now, Mort, you must sleep on the front side, for the shingle nails come through the boards of the roof, and if you should forget, and jump up on end, they'd stick right into your skull."

"They are not long enough to go through."

"Probably not through a skull so thick as yours, but they would draw blood, and might give you a headache."

When they awoke in the morning, Rich said, "Mort, I can spend the whole forenoon with you, but in the afternoon they will need me at the shop. In the evening we can be together again."

When breakfast was over, Morton said, "Rich, what are your plans for the future? Have you decided in respect to a profession? for I don't suppose you really intend to pass your life at the anvil, after spending so many years and so much money getting an education."

"It would not be so much of a sacrifice as you may suppose, and if I had not been through college, I would do so, for I love to work iron; it comes as natural as water to a duck. Do you go up and look over my books while I split up some oven wood, and then I'll tell you."

"I'll help you split the wood."

"Come on."

"Rich, who was that old lady at the breakfast table?"

"Aunt Blunt, mother's aunt. Didn't they introduce you? She came last night, before we came home, and went to bed."

"I thought your mother's name was Lucy; but this morning the old lady called her Mary."

"Mother's name is Mary L.; Mary Lucy. The Lucy is for my great aunt, and she always calls her so, but we call her Lucy. One of my sisters is named Mary B., after mother and the Blunts."

CHAPTER XII.
DID NOT COME TO SEE THE WRECK.

Returning to the garret, Rich said, "About a profession—is it?" flinging himself on the bed, while Morton, seated in a chair, thrust his feet out of the window. "Just have the goodness to open that volume on the table."

It was Bell's Operative Surgery.

"Then you are going to study medicine?"

"It is registered on leaves of brass."

"When did you decide?"

"I've been trying to decide ever since I left college; but I did decide before I left the breakfast table the morning father told me the boom and mills had gone. I borrowed these books of our doctor, and at night, when I'm not too tired, I read them once in the while; when work permits I go with him to visit some patient. I went with him a week ago when he amputated a man's hand at the wrist. He is very kind, has large practice, and rides long distances, as he has the practice of this and the next town."

"You won't accomplish much in this way."

"I don't expect to; but I can't leave father now, as I find that my taking hold has been a great help and comfort to him and my uncle. They have a good deal of work, and it is increasing every day; and I don't mean to leave them till I see the family in more comfortable quarters. The shop and house adjoining was my grandfather's, and when my father failed, passed into the hands of a Mr. Montague. He gives my father the use of the shop and tools, and in the fall, when the family now in it moves out, will let him have the old house, which is an excellent one, built by my grandfather after he acquired property. My father and uncle are living in this old shell, working incessantly. When no other work comes in, my uncle, who can work in wood as well as iron, makes wheels. My father puts on the tires. They sell them. Mother takes in spinning, and saves every cent. I do all I can in order to be able, at the end of the summer, to buy back grandfather's tools, that we may have something of our own. Besides, they are dear to father. He helped make most of them when he was a boy, and says there's a history to every one of them."

"How long is it going to take to do all that?"

"Not longer than September or the middle of October, if we are all well. In the mean time I shall read what medicine I can, go round with Dr. Jones occasionally, and when I see the family in the new house and comfortable, take an academy somewhere or high school, and teach till I can earn money enough to go on with my studies."

"You're a good boy, Rich."

"Why don't you tell me some news?"

"I'm going to. That *academy* is all ready."

"What do you mean by that?"

"Did you think I would leave my studies and come way up here just to look at the wreck? Put my arm round your neck, whimper, and say, What a pity!"

"Explain, Mort, please, that's a good fellow."

"Who said I wasn't a good fellow? Well, Perk's got an academy for you in the next town to his whenever you're ready to take it, salary two hundred a year. He fitted for college there, knows all the trustees, and everybody in town; and he's cracked you up sky high; told all the boys what a nice fellow you are, the most lovable man ever God made, the trustees what a splendid classical scholar you are, and all the young ladies how handsome. So I advise you, as a sincere friend, to take unto yourself nitre and much soap, and wash off that smut, which seems to me to be under the skin."

"O, Mort, this is all *your* work!"

"No,'tain't; it's all old Perk's. I only came to tell the news."

"But you were the *means* of it."

"No; it was that good Being whom you, after so many years of prosperity, couldn't afford to think about or thank till he sent the river to put you in mind of him."

"How can I ever thank you enough?"

"Do you think a man ought to be thanked for helping himself?"

"No, of course not."

"Are not you and I one? Didn't you say only last night we were one, and that there never was a shadow between us? What are you talking about?"

"I can't understand how they can wait my leisure. There must of course be a definite time when the term begins."

"Certainly; Perk will send you a catalogue; but he will take the school till you come. I told him I knew something about your affairs, and thought it doubtful if you could come at the first part of the term."

"This is a kind of joyous time, Mort; makes this old attic seem real pleasant."

"Yes; the architecture is simple in design; but the atmosphere is most exhilarating."

"I suppose I can tell father and mother?"

"To be sure. A good story is no worse for being twice told."

"What is Perk doing?"

"Just what you were doing all last year."

After dinner Rich went to the shop, and Morton, first taking a long walk, called there on his way back, and found Mr. Robert alone.

"Where is Rich?" he asked.

"Well, a man came here to get a 'clevis' pin made, and let them take his horse and wagon to haul a load of coal, while I made the pin. You seem to think a good deal of Rich, as you call him, Mr. Morton."

"I don't know how I could love him any more than I do."

"Well, he's a boy that deserves to be thought of. He never was brought up to do the leastest individual thing, 'cept to study a book and make some little gimcrank with tools; and yet to see how he took hold the moment his father's misfortunes came—went right to the anvil, never murmured or complained; and though he's my nephew, I *will* say that he's worth as much to-day in this shop as the general run of apprentices that have worked two years; and as for working in wood, he always took to that. 'Twas born in him."

"Don't you think, Mr. Richardson, that a boy whose grandfather and father were blacksmiths is more likely to be handy in a shop?"

"I suppose these things are kind of handed down. I know there's a good deal in the blood; I know it by our girls. They are all broken down, sit and sigh, think what they used to have, and let their mother do all the work."

"Are they not own sisters to Rich?"

"The same father and mother; but they take back after the Armstrongs; they don't take after the Richardsons, who are a resolute, stirring breed of folks. Their old grandmother Armstrong was a dreadful slack-twisted, shiftless woman; had to be helped by the town; and when the selectmen gave her a cord of wood, she'd put about two foot into the great fireplace, declare she'd have one fire if she died for it, and then sit, fold her hands in her lap, and enjoy it. Her children took after her, 'cept my brother's wife, and she's smart as steel; took after her mother's people, the Blunts. But that old woman that's been dead and buried this twenty years has come out in the grandchildren. It is not the way, Mr. Morton, to bring up children. This twenty years past I've been saying to Clem and Lucy that they were doing wrong by their children. Says I, 'Bring them up to work as we were. If they don't need to, it's the easiest thing in the world to leave off; but it's hard to learn.' Then Lucy would say, 'Uncle, I don't want them to have to work as hard as I have.' Says I, 'Perhaps they may be obliged to. What then?' Then Clem would laugh, and say that old maids' and old bachelors' children were always brought up right."

"But I'm sure Rich has come out well."

"Indeed he has; but he is a remarkable boy, and is no rule to go by. Besides, we must thank you, and do thank you, for a good part of that: you did a parent's duty by him. Don't you think he is in better shape to keep the 'cademy, for teaching school in college, and wasn't he in better shape, and would he have had the pluck to go so willingly to the anvil if he hadn't been broke in by you in college?"

"I suppose you are right, Mr. Richardson; but in respect to the young ladies."

"Call 'em girls, Mr. Morton; and they are not very young at that."

"Well, girls, then. Would any training their parents could have given taken the thin blood (the *Armstrong*, as you call it) out of them."

"I don't suppose it would; but it would have helped it amazingly. You see if I get a bar of Swedish iron, first rate, stamped 'Hoop L,' I put it into the fire, and work it without fear; but if I have a bar of English iron, brash and coarse, can't get any better, and must work it up, why, by taking great pains, heating it just right, and working it just right, I can, by coaxing, make it answer—not so good a purpose as the other iron, but can make it very useful. That's the way with children; you've got 'em, and got to work 'em up, and must make the best of 'em, as I do with 'brash' iron. These girls were partly on our side the house, and if they had been put right to it, it would have helped the better part, and kept the other back, just as the saw-makers put the nature into a saw by hammering when it has been softened in grinding. Now all they do is to put the dishes on the table, sweep up the hearth and look In the glass, wring their hands, and tell about what *used* to be. They might teach school if they only had 'sprawl' enough."

Mr. Richardson then told Morton that his brother would take an apprentice when they moved into the old homestead and had room, after which Rich would be able to leave home.

CHAPTER XIII.
MORTON'S BUSINESS.

Morton set out for Portland the next morning, leaving Rich glad and grateful, and in the best of spirits himself, arising from the conviction that better days were in store both for Rich and his parents. He took his seat on the box, and was still more confirmed in this opinion by the conversation with the driver, of whom he had inquired the way to Mr. Richardson's shop the afternoon of his arrival.

"Then you didn't have any trouble finding Richardson's shop t'other day: git, git, git along there, you white horse."

"No, I found it without the least difficulty."

"Thought you would. Belong in these parts? What you 'bout there, old Dick?" Crack, crack, crack!

"No, I belong up back of Portland."

"Buxton, praps."

"No."

"Maybe you're from Conway."

"Thereabouts."

"Fine men them ere two Richardsons."

"Yes, but they have met with a great misfortune."

"That's so; and it's made a great stir and talk, and a great feelin'; for they was two men that was master sot by in this place, and desarved to be; folks are both glad and sorry."

"I shouldn't think people would be glad if they were generally liked."

"Well, that's what I call a kernondrum. Ha, ha!—Whey there, Tom; what you foolin' for?—People ain't glad that they lost their property; no, no; everybody's sorry for that, and they could hire any amount of money, and go on again, if they would; but you see they're the greatest blacksmiths; there never was anybody in these parts could temper any kind of an edge tool like as Clement Richardson, 'cept his old dad afore him; and he, they said, took it up in his own head. You take notice 'tis born in 'em, same as a cat carries her navigation in her head. So people say, 'Now Clem Richardson has gone to work agin, we shall have good tools;' and so they feel kind of glad about that ere. They'll have a master sight of work as soon as it's known round, and they'll rise again. Squire Walker says 'they're bound to.' I heard him tell Dr. Jones. 'Quainted with Dr. Jones?"

"I haven't that pleasure."

"First-rate man. I heard him say with my own ears (that is, the squire), says he, 'Doctor, you can't kill one of them Richardsons, not if you cut their head off,' and the doctor, he says, 'The young sprig, that's been thought to be a sort of baby, is jest as good grit as the old ones, and comes right up to the collar.' Them isn't jestly his words, but that's the upshot on 'em. Then there's two of 'em, and they can carry on both parts of the work. There's only one family to support, 'cause Bob's an old bach, and they're not only brothers in name, but in natur, are well matched, and step alike, jest like them ere leaders of mine; about as good going horses as a man need wish to drive. Reckon you're some kin to the Richardsons."

"No, none at all."

"Maybe you're sparkin' one of the gals."

"No, I never had the courage."

"Reckon you're a college-larnt man, like young Richardson; praps you're a doctor or lawyer, or some sich."

"No, I'm in a *business*."

"Du tell. What kind of a business?"

"One that pays the best the closer it's followed."

"I reckon that's so with most all business."

"I've invented something—something that will make my fortune."

"Maybe you'd be willing to tell a feller what it is."

"It is a hog-sty that will fat hogs without corn."

"Massy sakes! How does it do it?"

"That's the secret."

"On course you'll make a lot; that's the master. How many on 'em you sold in this town?"

"I haven't got to work yet."

The next day the story was all over town that the stranger who was visiting at Richardson's was worth a mint of money, that he had invented a hog-sty to fat hogs without corn, and came to offer himself to Mary Richardson, but his courage failed, and he went off without doing it.

What a pity! people said: it would have been such a nice thing for the Richardsons, just as they were situated.

A good many thought Rich would write to the young man, and invite him to come again.

At this period the country around the head waters of the rivers was one unbroken forest. The lumbering operations, previous to this, had extended but a short distance from the sea-coast; but now vast numbers of men and teams were sent into the woods in all directions. The character of Clement Richardson as a superior axe and edge-tool maker was well known everywhere, and the news that he had resumed work soon spread among the lumbermen who were laying their plans and arranging to put teams into the woods the coming winter.

As early as the tenth of July orders for axes began to pour in upon the Richardsons. The mills formerly belonging to them, shattered in the freshet, were repaired, and new ones built upon the sites of those entirely destroyed, occasioning a good deal of blacksmith work, as new mill-chains, dogs, hooks, bands, bolts, and pintles were to be made. Horse and ox-shoeing, and carriage work, also increased with the increase of business.

The result of this was, that Andrew Montague enlarged the shop, built two new chimneys and forges, and the Richardsons not only bought the old tools, but also two pairs of bellows, anvils and other tools, for the new forges. They now moved into their father's old house, vacated by Coleman, hired journeymen and took two apprentices, Clement giving his attention entirely to the manufacture of edge tools, and Robert to horse-shoeing and carriage work, ox-shoeing and tiring of heavy wheels. The Richardsons now found themselves in comfortable circumstances; they had a good house rent free, as Montague absolutely refused to receive any rent, either for the house or shop, until the expiration of a year from the time of occupancy, saying that they would want one year to get fairly started, and all their money to buy coal, iron, and tools.

In consequence of this increase of work, Rich was able to leave home sooner than he had supposed possible at the period of Morton's visit, and accordingly wrote to Perk that he would be with him in a week after the commencement of the fall term.

He found Perk at the public house, waiting to welcome him, as the stage drove up about sundown. It was the first time they had met since the morning they left Radcliffe Hall. Our readers, who are apprised of the relations existing between these two boys in college, and the temperament of each, can imagine the nature of the greeting. It is sufficient to say that it was not remarkably formal. This, however, was not in the least objectionable to a band of academy boys (who, in expectation of his arrival, had assembled to have a look at their new teacher, and whom Perk now presented to Rich as a portion of his scholars), if we may judge from the talk among themselves as they went away, arm-in-arm, a boy every now and then breaking rank, and walking backwards, those at the end of the file keeping about two steps in advance, in order to face the rest, and impress their own sentiments more forcibly upon their companions of less sanguine temperaments.

They were scarcely out of ear-shot, when Dan Clemens, breaking with a jump from the midst, and walking backwards, with one hand on the shoulder of Ned Baker, and the other on that of Frank Merrill, shouted as though he was afraid some other would get the start of him,—

"Ned, Frank, all of you! I know I shall like that man; can't help liking him. I'm *bound* to like him."

"I'm the same way!" shouted Horace Williams from the extreme right. "Didn't you see, boys, how he and Mr. Perkins caught hold of each other? That's what took me down. There's some soul in that man, I tell you."

"O, he's a bully man!" roared Clinton Blanchard from the extreme left; "a fellow can tell by the looks of him; he shows it right out in his face."

"You might know he's a first-rate man," cried Phil Greely; "else Mr. Perkins wouldn't love him so. I thought I never should like anybody else as Master Perkins; but I guess this man is just like him, and I mean to tell all the fellows I know."

By this time, as boy after boy kept stepping out, they had got into a circle, and further progress was necessarily arrested: not so, however, the expression of opinions.

"He has not a very scholarly look," said Edward Randolph, who was a very proper boy; "not at all the air of a close student. His hands are rough and hard; he hurt me when he shook my hand."

"You shut up,—will you?" retorted Dan. "You've got the dyspepsy."

"No, I haven't, neither."

"Well, you want to have it," said Frank Merrill.

It was evident that in respect to popularity among these boys, the star of Rich was in the ascendant, and before nine o'clock the next morning they had brought the rest of the school to the same opinion.

First impressions go a great way with all persons, especially with the young. Had Rich gone deliberately to work to win the hearts of his future scholars, he could have devised no method so effectual as this unconscious manifestation of his true nature in their presence.

"The first thing for me to do, Perk," said Rich, "is to look up a boarding-place; till that is done I shall stay here."

"No, you won't stay here; you are not going to stop here; you are going home with me to stop, to-night, at my boarding-place, and I think you will conclude to remain there."

When they reached the house, Perk introduced Rich to the mistress of it, who he at the same time informed him was his aunt.

A few minutes after they sat down to supper, her son came, in whom Rich recognized Dan Clemens, one of the boys Perk had introduced to him at the *tavern*. Hotels were not in fashion in that section of Maine.

After the repast they went to Perk's room. The first thing that attracted the attention of Rich was a large picture hung over the mantle-piece.

"I should like to know, Perk, where you got that."

"Stole it out of Mort's desk. I was afraid if I didn't he'd give it to you; but I told him of it, and he gave it to me afterwards. Isn't that something to call up old friends and old associations?" It was the original sketch of James Trafton as a negro, drawn at midnight by Morton in Radcliffe.

"It is so, Perk. How that brings the whole thing back! It seems to me I can see you scrubbing his face, that was as white as your own, with soap and ashes, and hear him say, 'Does it come off, Perk?'"

"I tell you what tickled me most, Rich—to see Savage spreading ink on that poultice, and Trafton thinking it came off his own face."

"Those were pleasant days, Perk; but they can come back only in recollection; and I feel like applying to that production of Mort's the language of Burns,—

'Thou mind'st me of departed joys,

Departed never to return.'"

"Rich, kick off your boots and put on these slippers." Rich obeyed. "Now put on this study-gown."

Perk then pulled a lounge up to the fire, and they sat down to talk.

After reviewing the past, which old class-mates are as sure to do as is an old sailor to overhaul his chest, and take everything out of it (sometimes a very light job), as soon as he gets to sea, Perk said,—

"I didn't expect you so soon, Rich."

"I was able to leave sooner than I expected when I wrote you. Might, indeed, have come before; but it took me a week to clean up. Look at these." He spread out his hands, that were hard, the palms and the edges of the forefingers and thumbs a rusty brown, and cracked.

"It is not dirt, but stains from iron and from coal dust; and that, too, after using on them a quart of linseed oil, not to mention vinegar, soap, and rye meal."

"How are you pleased with my aunt, Rich?"

"Very much indeed. The boy at table is one of those I met at the stage tavern. Is he your cousin?"

"Yes, and a downright good boy he is, too, and a real comfort to my aunt, who is a widow. He is dead in love with you."

"Perhaps he will change his mind; boys are not wont to cherish a very fervent love for teachers."

"You'll find yourself mistaken in that respect. Dan, and a crony of his, Horace Williams, will take to you, and cling to you, just as Ned Austin and Will Montgomery did to you and Mort. You can stimulate them, and they will leap under it as a high-spirited horse catches the excitement of its rider, especially if he loves him."

CHAPTER XIV.
WINNING GOLDEN OPINIONS.

"In the morning, Perk, I want you to help me about finding a boarding-place, or some room that I can hire cheap, and board myself. I should prefer a garret, as that will be the cheapest. There"—laying a two-dollar bill on the table—"is every cent of money I possess in the world; and if I study medicine I must have books, that come very high, instruments by and by, and instruction from an experienced physician. I am, to be sure, well clothed. I have clothing sufficient, with economy, to last for years, but money I have none."

"I know I am not capable of giving you advice, and cannot expect that you will receive it from me as you would from Mort; but I beg of you, whatever you do, don't go to starving yourself; it will be a losing game in the end. If you are going to work hard all day in school, and then study when out of it, you need, and must have, good, nourishing food, and plenty of it. There was Eckford, of our class, lived on water gruel and molasses, and roast potatoes, and made out to graduate. But what did he ever amount to, more than sweetened water?"

"He never was more than half alive, to begin with. I am in good case, and must economize the last cent."

"Economize, with a vengeance! Saving at the tap, and spilling at the bung-hole. A precious doctor you'll make. Going to dry up the juices, both of body and brain, by starvation. Now let me plan. My aunt has considerable land and other property, and needs some one to aid her in the care of it. Dan is a mere boy, and it brings a good deal of care upon her. If you will see to her affairs, cut the wood, take care of the garden in the summer (Dan milks, and takes care of the cow and horse), keep her accounts, and just do what pertains to the house (if there is anything beyond that, she will hire other help), you can stay in this room, have your board, fuel, and a horse to ride occasionally, you can borrow medical books of Dr. Ryan, practice on my aunt, who is in delicate health, dearly loves to take medicine, wears a Burgundy pitch plaster between her shoulders, reads Buchan's Domestic Medicine, and Parson Meek will pray for you. I think this will be a great deal better than your starvation plan, unless you think it would be derogatory to your character, and injure your influence as principal of the academy, if it should be known that you cut wood and did chores."

"Derogatory!" cried Rich, jumping up. "I don't value the opinion of any who think honest labor derogatory *that*," snapping his fingers. "If they don't like it, they may dislike it. I can earn as much at the anvil as I can here, and all the reason I prefer it is, I can study when I have done my day's work here; and after I have been at work in the shop all day I am tired and sleepy. I will most gladly fall in with the offer of your aunt, and do all or anything she wants done."

"Rich, you are no more like a fellow we used to call *Rich* in Radcliffe, than chalk's like cheese."

"I've been through a 'discipline,' as President Appleton would say. Then, I used to dip my fingers in rose water of a morning, and dress my hair with pomatum. Since that, I've had to wash in an iron-hooped bucket, and wipe on a tow towel cousin german to a nutmeg grater. Sweat and coal dust have taken the place of pomatum. It didn't last, however, longer than the first term of the freshman year. I caught an expression on Mort's face one day, when I was fixing up before the glass, that made me, as soon as his back was turned, fling the rose water and pomatum into the slop pail. I tell you, Perk, there's no tonic equal to iron. I mean to give lots of it when I am a doctor."

"So I think; but I like to take it best in the shape of a gun barrel, a fish-hook, or a pair of skates."

The number of pupils in the academy was quite large, and, as was customary in those days, they consisted of both sexes, ranging in age from ten to nineteen, and even twenty years. There were boys fitting for college, and others pursuing English studies. Some of the older scholars studied surveying, book-keeping, and navigation.

Rich gave himself wholly to his work, and speedily created among his scholars not merely an attachment to himself, but enthusiasm in study, and desire to excel. It was soon evident, both to the trustees and more advanced scholars, that their present teacher was greatly superior in every department, not only to Perk, but any instructor who had preceded him.

The fact that he did chores, and attended to business matters, in order to defray the expense of his board, so far from proving derogatory, as Perk had hinted, operated in precisely the opposite manner. Had he resorted to this method of reducing his expenses from penuriousness, and an overweening desire to accumulate, such, doubtless, would have been the result, and the proceeding would have excited both ridicule and contempt.

The instincts of the boys, however, divined that this was not his character. They felt themselves drawn towards him by that magnetic influence that his college mates confessed, and were proud of his scholarship and commanding ability, that even those who could not appreciate felt. In addition to this they were not long in discovering that, although he did chores, and even cleaned out the pig-sty, he was the best dressed man in the town on the Sabbath, which was to them a sore puzzle. But when it leaked out, probably through Perk, that he had been reared in affluence, was now flung upon his own resources, struggling to obtain a professional education, and that his style of dress was merely the remnant of better days, and not occasioned by mere love of display, the knowledge produced universal sympathy and respect, the whole community vying with each other in the manifestation of it.

Although practising the most rigid economy, husbanding every moment of time, and performing a great deal of labor, the noble nature of Rich manifested itself in a thousand ways; and strange it is how this unwritten, unspoken language of the heart is generally felt and understood. He was patient with the dull, encouraged the industrious, and stimulated to the utmost those scholars possessed of superior ability, while the mere desire to merit his esteem and affection roused indolent and wayward boys to persevering effort, and inspired them with a love of study and spirit of emulation they had never felt before.

But when Granny Fluker (after he went into the blacksmith's shop, made a new crank to her flax wheel, mended the cover of her Dutch oven, that was broke in two, by drilling holes in it, and putting wrought iron cleats across, fastened with rivets, and made a new bail to the oven) exclaimed, "God bless the young gentleman for condescending to sich a poor old worn-out critter as I am, that have to be helped by the town. Well, it's allers the way, in this world; them what's got the biggest hearts to do allers have the least to do *with*. But if the prayers of a poor old lone body like me can do him any good, he'll sartain have 'em."

She expressed the universal sentiment of the whole community.

To increase still more the estimation in which Rich was held, it was ascertained that he was an excellent singer. The parish choir was in a most wretched condition. A maiden lady, who had long been distinguished as a singer, began to show unmistakable signs of age, and her voice cracked. She received from the younger members sundry hints to leave. These she took in high dudgeon, and left, together with a brother and two sisters, who were fine singers, and who espoused her quarrel. Before the new members who were introduced upon their leaving could be drilled, the chorister, who had made a great part of the disturbance, left town, taking his bass-viol with him.

In this condition of things, Rich was invited to take the lead of the choir, and accepted, established choir meetings, and soon put matters to rights; while the refractory brother and his two sisters, finding that they were not necessary, got over their huff, and came back.

The younger portion of the choir, ascertaining from Dan Clemens that Rich played the violin, persuaded him to bring it to church the next Sunday. The moment Rich drew the bow across the strings, Deacon Starkweather got up, slamming the pew door after him, left the church, and going into the pasture, out of sight and sound of the ungodly thing, sat down on a stump, in a snow-storm, till he judged it was time for the sermon to begin, when he returned, as he had no quarrel with Parson Meek, and merely wished to show his displeasure, and enter a protest against the fiddle. Rich, however, smoothed all asperities, and reconciled the worthy deacon, by persuading the members of the parish most interested in music to purchase a bass-viol, upon which he performed to the satisfaction of all; Deacon Starkweather inviting Rich, and all the members of the choir, to tea, when he explained to them that he had never cherished the least hardness against any member of the choir, but that his action was in reference to the *instrument*, and the associations connected with that exponent of folly, and concluded with a most generous contribution toward the purchase of the bass-viol. Thus was the affair that at one time threatened to break up the parish most happily settled. Rich earned the reputation of a peacemaker, and young man of excellent judgment, and the deacon, through his device delivered from an uncomfortable position (as his conduct by no means met with general approbation), became the staunch friend of Rich, declaring, upon every proper occasion, that "he was a young man that had the root of the matter in him."

The period at which Rich began the study of medicine was the commencement of a great revolution in medical theory and practice, both in relation to the treatment of disease and surgery; young and earnest men were struggling in every direction for light; new discoveries were made, reverence for the past was gradually wearing off, and the old theories of practice were subjected to a most searching and often irreverent scrutiny.

Dr. Ryan by no means belonged to that class of mind sometimes designated by the term, "The sword frets out the scabbard." On the other hand, he was hale and hearty, possessed of a noble frame, hair slightly tinged with gray, but ruddy cheeks, a fine set of teeth of pearly whiteness, and a frank, hearty manner, betokening real goodness of heart.

Though possessed of very moderate abilities, the doctor was a man of sterling worth, great integrity, and kind and sympathizing nature. He enjoyed a large practice, being the only physician in the place. The poor loved him, because he was ever as ready to attend to their wants as to those of his more wealthy patients, often put shoes on the feet of a barefooted child, and did not hesitate to bestow flannels and fuel, when he felt that they were more necessary than medicine. The utmost confidence was reposed in him, as his more intelligent patients, if disposed to doubt his skill in difficult cases, knew perfectly well that he would not hesitate a moment in calling in more competent persons, when he felt their aid was required.

At this period the spirit of inquiry was abroad. There were rumors in the air, and forebodings of a radical reform in medical practice. Practitioners of the doctor's age, who were either too indolent, prejudiced, or too far advanced in life to receive and act upon new ideas, were by no means to be envied, being somewhat in the position of one upon a ledge in the sea, cut off by the tide, that, constantly rising, rendered his passing into oblivion merely a question of time.

The old physicians stigmatized these disturbers of the peace of antiquity and their own as quacks, new lights, upstarts, and utterly unsafe as experimenters with human life. The advocates of the improved practice, on the other hand, were by no means backward in denouncing their seniors as fossils, petrifactions, enemies to all progress, and only desirous of retailing drugs at ninety per cent. profit, and fattening the graveyards; of promoting gangrene, and needless amputations, through their ignorance of the first principles of surgery; multiplying cripples by malpractice and ignorance of anatomy; that they had one mode of treatment for all disorders; and the time-honored allusion to "Procrustes' bed" was lavishly applied to their opponents.

The good doctor, firmly wedded to the ancient practice, felt all the animosity his genial nature permitted him to indulge in respect to the new lights; and when he heard that a young man thoroughly impregnated (as he could not doubt) with radical notions, was about to take the academy, and had already commenced the study of medicine, he felt very much as an old crower, who has walked in state, and lorded it over his dames, might be supposed to feel when he sees a young rooster suddenly flung down in the barn-yard, and inwardly resolved that the young upstart should receive neither aid, comfort, nor countenance from him.

CHAPTER XV.
HOW DAN TOOK HIS MEDICINE.

While in this irritable and pugnacious temper it chanced most fortunately that the doctor did not happen to fall in with Rich; and when he did, being in a different state of mind, matters wore quite another aspect.

The doctor was remarkably fond of music, and no mean performer himself upon the clarionet. Being at meeting for the first time since the arrival of Rich on the Sabbath when Deacon Starkweather made his exit, he was mightily tickled with the whole proceedings; said the deacon ought to have his head shaved, and a blister drawn on it, and was consequently inclined to feel more kindly disposed towards Rich. While his prejudices were thus somewhat weakened, he was introduced to the latter by Perk, and was so much charmed with the modest appearance, intelligence, and address of Rich, that he received him with all the cordiality of a parent.

"This young gentleman, Mr. Perkins," said the doctor to Perk the next morning, "is a very different person from the great majority of those who profess to study medicine, having some respect for age and experience, and as amendable to counsel as he is intelligent and refined in his manners."

The doctor was not dependent upon his practice for a living, having inherited an ample property from his grandfather. His library was large, consisting of all the medical works then esteemed, and a complete set of the instruments then used in this country. It is safe to say that the doctor consulted the length of his purse in the choice of books, rather than his mental needs, as Rich, after looking over, found a great portion of them with the leaves still uncut, although they had been ten, and some of them twenty, years in the doctor's possession.

Most physicians at that period were provided with more or less bones for the study of anatomy, generally of the limbs, as they were most liable to be broken or dislocated: very few went beyond this. Dr. Ryan, however, had not even all these—only the bones of the lower extremities; but the deficiency was in some manner supplied by plates contained in the anatomical works in his library; indeed, he felt very little interest in surgery, dreading nothing so much as being called to set a bone, amputate a limb, or reduce a dislocation, and frequently advised his patients to send for Dr. Slaughter, who excelled as a surgeon.

In the course of his long practice, he had rendered many cripples for life by sheer carelessness in bandaging limbs that had been properly set, and once made a blunder that would have proved fatal to one less beloved.

He was called to a man who had recently moved into the place, who was afflicted with a tumor in his ham; the doctor, after examining, shoved his lancet into it. To his terror and astonishment, the blood spurted in his face; he had cut an artery! The new lights represented that he was so frightened the patient bled to death while he sent for his instruments. It was not so; yet not much better. The doctor clapped his thumb on the artery, and instructed the family to arrest the blood, in the meanwhile sent for his instruments and took up the artery; but the coats of the artery, where he applied the ligature, being diseased, sloughed in the night; and in a short time the ligature came away, and the man bled to death.

It was an old false aneurism, in which so many concentric layers of coagulum had accumulated that no pulsation could be perceived. Had the doctor inquired into the history of it, he would have found that it had pulsated in the past; but neglecting to do this, and unable to perceive the throb of the artery, he mistook it for an abscess. Notwithstanding his lack of surgical skill, he was versed in the properties and operation of medicines, a close observer, could detect the nature of disease, and had acquired a great amount of experimental knowledge.

He made an agreement with Rich to superintend his studies, permit him the use of his library, with opportunities to visit patients, for thirty dollars a year.

It was now that Rich began to realize the deep-seated affection cherished for him by his scholars. There were many young men, the sons of farmers, from nineteen to twenty-one, who attended the academy in the winter term; in March they came together, and cut up the whole year's stock of wood for Mrs. Clemens, and put it under cover, thus relieving Rich, and affording him time for study. Dan Clemens and his mates also performed their part in smaller matters, so that Rich had really no more to do than sufficed for exercise.

There could not be a greater contrast than existed between Rich, earnest, ambitious, still farther stimulated by the pressure of poverty, and the genial old doctor, who loved a good story and a good joke, had an abundance of this world's goods, and cared very little whether his practice increased or decreased, so that it was not intruded upon by the new lights.

Yet they were great friends. Rich loved the doctor, though soon made aware of his deficiencies, and treated him with the greatest deference; while the latter obstinately shut his eyes to the fact, often brought to view by his fellow-physician, Dr. Slaughter, that he was nourishing a most thorough-going radical and new light in his own bosom, although never obtruding his heresies; for if ever there was a boy bound to go to the root of principles, that boy was Rich.

Mrs. Clemens was a lady after the doctor's own heart. She was intelligent, refined, benevolent, and universally esteemed. Like most persons in delicate health, she was fond of having a physician round her, consulted the doctor in respect to every trifling indisposition, and was very conservative in her notions. She had one weak point, as who has not. This was a perfect passion for reading medical works and practising upon herself and the members of her family—a sentiment fostered by her delicate state of health.

This rendered it quite difficult for her to keep a hired girl, for though they liked her, and received good wages, they were not fond of the medicines she insisted upon their taking to keep them from being sick. Next to the Holy Scriptures, she reverenced Buchan's Domestic Medicine,—a copy of which, elegantly bound, lay on her table beside the Bible,—abhorred innovations in medical practice, and would much rather have died under the hands of a regular physician than been cured by a quack.

"Doctor," she said, one day, "how mysterious it seems, that my dear husband, who was a great, stout, healthy man, the very picture of health, and used to take care of me just like a baby, should be in his grave, and I still spared!"

"Invalids, ma'am, live the longest of any people in the world."

"How can that be, doctor?"

"Because they take care of themselves."

The good lady, indeed, took excellent care of herself; but she was sadly tried in regard to taking care of her son Dan.

Dan was a robust, red-cheeked boy, sound to the core, of fearless, sanguine temperament, and it was the hardest work in the world for Dan to sit on a bench and apply himself to study. Nothing but their attachment to Rich would have induced him and his sworn friends, Ned Baker and Frank Merrill, to attempt and accomplish it. But much as Dan loved his mother, he did abhor medicine, and to be coddled up.

Richardson was often placed between the two horns of a dilemma, as Mrs. Clemens invariably appealed to him when Dan proved refractory.

One morning his mother insisted that he had taken cold, and Dan as stoutly maintained the negative.

"Daniel, you must wear your great coat to school; your face is flushed, and I think you are feverish."

"It's always flushed, mother. I haven't one mite of cold, and I can't stand it to wear a coat this pleasant morning."

"Yes, you must, dear; your tongue is coated. I'll ask Mr. Richardson."

But Rich, who had overheard the conversation, made a bolt for the door, and escaped that time. In the course of an hour, Betty Gookins, the help, came in, bringing in her hand a garment.

"Only look here, ma'am. I went to pump a pail of water, and I couldn't, cause Dan's coat was in the pump-nose."

"O, dear, how that boy does try me! Well, I shall soon be in my grave."

But as the good lady had said the same for the last thirty years, there was evidently hope in the case. Dan, however, was not to escape so easily the watchful care of his mother. That night, when he came in to supper, he was regaled with the odor of salts and senna simmering in the corner.

"O, dear!" he said to himself; "have I got to take that awful, sickish, nasty stuff?"

The next morning, about half an hour before school-time, Rich wanted Dan.

"The poor child is not well, Mr. Richardson, and has gone into the unfinished room to take some medicine. He says he can take it better if he is alone, and nobody looking at him. I wish he didn't dislike to take medicine so much; if it was not such a trial to him, I should give him 'picra.'"

When Rich entered the room, Dan had got up a brick in the hearth, and was administering the salts and senna to the cross-sill beneath. He started like a guilty thing when the door opened, but, seeing who it was, completed his purpose.

"What are you about, Daniel?"

"Taking salts and senna, sir."

"Is that the way you always take them?"

"I never took any so before; but this is the way I mean to take them for the future. I expect to pour gallons into this hole."

"Are you well enough to get me a big log out of the wood-pile?"

"Certainly, Mr. Richardson. I never was weller in my life."

"But your mother said yesterday that your tongue was coated."

"So it was. I had been breaking a pan of cream. Mother don't like to have her cream disturbed after it is set. I licked the cream off my lips, but left it on my tongue."

"I think your mother'll have the best of it if she gives you salts and senna. She thinks highly of assafœtida, and may give you that."

"I never will take that; I'll leave home first."

The next evening, as Rich was passing through the kitchen with an armful of wood for his evening fire, he noticed Mrs. Clemens seated before the fire, in her lap a pair of old-fashioned kitchen bellows, on a chair beside her a skillet full of hot coals, a roll of sheep-skin, a junk of Burgundy pitch, and a knife. After cutting from the skin a piece of the right size for a plaster, she placed on it a piece of the pitch, put both on the flat side of the bellows, made the knife hot in the coals, and spread the plaster; while Dan, with no very joyous expression of countenance, sat awaiting the result.

"I am going to put this plaster between Daniel's shoulders, Mr. Richardson," said she; "it is a sovereign remedy for a cold; doesn't open the pores like a sweat, and expose one to take more cold."

The next morning the good lady declared the plaster had worked wonders; that Daniel's cold was very much better, and would soon be well.

"Perhaps I had better take it off, my son, wipe it, and wipe the perspiration from your back. The plaster will draw better, and it will prevent its itching and annoying you in school."

"O, no, mother; I shall be late. It don't itch one mite."

And he rushed from the house.

"It is very singular," replied his mother, looking after him, "*my* plasters always itch, and are very troublesome. I think they don't do much good except they itch."

Mrs. Clemens would have been less surprised had she known that the plaster began to itch the moment Dan was warm in bed. After enduring it awhile, he pulled it off and tucked it up chimney. So he told Frank Merrill, with whom, on the way to school, he shared some guava jelly given him by his mother, after taking the salts and senna, to take the taste out of his mouth.

CHAPTER XVI.
PERIL OF BEING OUT EVENINGS.

Directly upon commencing the study of anatomy, Rich began to feel the need of something more than the plates contained in the books.

It was some distance to go, for the study of bones, to the doctor's house, and he wanted something that he could keep in his room, and have at hand to refer to; besides, the doctor had none of the bones of the trunk—only the skull and part of the limbs. He likewise wished to dissect and study muscles, tendons, the structure of skin, bone, veins, arteries, and internal organs, in their natural state, since for him to procure a human subject was at that time out of the question, as he was without means to purchase even a skeleton.

In these circumstances he conceived that much might be learned by a careful study and dissection of the bodies of animals in connection with the plates found in the books.

Mr. Clemens, the husband of Rich's landlady, owned and worked a large breadth of land, which necessitated the keeping of many horses, as he did all his farm work with horses; but after his decease the greater part of the land, and all the horses except one, were sold. On the lower floor of the stable was a small room, once devoted to storing and oiling harnesses, in which was a fireplace, and at one corner, a large closet without shelves, and very broad, where the more valuable riding harnesses, not in constant use, were hung, to defend them from dust. There were also some harness-maker's tools, old straps, thorough-braces, and a large leather boot, that had survived the vehicle to which it was once attached.

Fire-wood in those days was made but small account of, especially by Mrs. Clemens, who could not consume half of the decaying and downwood on her land.

"Mrs. Clemens," said Rich, "are you willing I should clear out the old harness-room, and make a fire there occasionally?"

"What for, Mr. Richardson? If you want more room in the house you can have it. It will certainly be more comfortable than the barn; besides, I am afraid you will take cold."

"Indeed, Mrs. Clemens, I need not hesitate to tell a lady of your respect for and appreciation of the medical profession, that as I proceed in my studies, I shall want to dissect and experiment upon the bodies of animals. You know that, although the courts and the community are ever ready to prosecute a physician to the extent of the law for a mistake in setting a bone, they throw every obstacle in the way of his obtaining any accurate knowledge of the machine he is expected to repair." The law in respect to this matter was more stringent then than at present.

"But, Mr. Richardson, if you should lose a mother, sister, or dear friend,— Mr. Perkins, for instance,—and had placed them in the earth, with all the respect nature dictates, could you bear to feel that they were taken from the grave, exposed upon a table, and cut to pieces by students smoking cigars, and laughing, and jesting, as though to fit and harden them for their profession by driving every spark of feeling and humanity out of their bosoms?"

"No, I could not. I don't believe, however, that there is the least necessity of this hardening process you have referred to; if I believed that, by devoting myself to the study of medicine, I should lose one particle of kindly feeling that I now possess, should harden my heart and curtail my sympathies, or change in any respect, except in obtaining self-command that I might discharge more efficiently my duty, I would relinquish study and go back to the anvil to-morrow. If a doctor is rough and unfeeling, it is to be attributed to his natural temper, and want of culture, not to his profession."

"Then I suppose you are just the one who ought to be a doctor, though I think it is strange that you should choose that profession. As I was telling Mrs. Merrill the other day, I observed you was so sensitive you never *could* do some of those dreadful things doctors were obliged to perform. But as for the harness-room, you may do whatever you like with it; there's a padlock in the house belongs to the outside door, and a key to the lock on the closet. If there is anything there worth saving, put it in the loft, and any old rubbish you can burn up."

"But the wood, I will pay for that."

"By no means, there's wood enough."

After clearing out the place, and cleansing it thoroughly, Rich made a table, and put iron rings into it, in order that he might fasten any animal that he wished to operate upon. He then procured buckles and waxed ends, and from the boot of the old chaise made straps of different lengths for the same purpose, and put a lock on the door in lieu of the padlock. As the stern, patient smith of the wilderness, amid the melancholy moan of pine forests, and the roar of the stream, wrought out by sheer pluck and perseverance, a mechanical trade, so his earnest grandson, completely absorbed in his chosen pursuit, strove to verify, by experiment upon the bodies of such animals as he could procure, the theories he studied.

In short, under the intoxication of a dominant impulse, he did things that, had they come to the knowledge of Mrs. Clemens, she would no longer have doubted of his adaptedness to the medical profession on the score of sensitiveness; so impervious to emotion in certain directions will an absorbing idea render a person otherwise most impressible.

He dissected frogs to observe the muscles of the thigh, and irritated the muscular tissue of animals, thus creating inflammation, in order to watch its progress. Though there are striking differences between the composition of man and the animal, still there is correspondence enough to admit of much being learned; and in default of a human subject, he resorted to this method, as his grandfather, unable to procure an anvil, made a stone answer the purpose. The lungs of a hog are very similar to those of a man, and he found no difficulty in procuring these. If a stray dog came along, he was most kindly welcomed by Rich; but it was observed that no stray dog, having once entered Mrs. Clemens's yard, was ever seen to come out again.

Marvelous was the industry of Rich, only equalled by his ingenuity. He soon had the large closet in the stable filled to overflowing with the skeletons of various animals he had dissected and wired together with great skill. He was much attached to Dan, who procured him animals to operate upon, while he, in turn mounted birds and squirrels for Dan—a matter in which Rich was very skilful.

He had been for a long time desirous of examining the structure of the eye, but could not procure a suitable subject. Mrs. Clemens possessed a cat of beautiful color and proportions, affectionate disposition, intelligent, and perfectly trained. Between this member of the family and Dan the affections of the good lady were about equally divided. When, as occasionally happened, Gertrude was unwell, the good lady was at her wits' end, as she would have nothing from Buchan, and eschewed Burgundy pitch plasters, salts, and senna. Indeed, she had much rather Dan would be sick, than Gertrude, for she knew what to do for Dan, while Gertrude would have nothing but catnip. At every meal she sat beside Mrs. Clemens in a high chair, and never offered to take anything from the table, waiting the leisure of her mistress. Dan also loved Gertrude dearly, and had taught her a great many tricks. Rich likewise conceived a fondness for the cat, being naturally fond of pets.

Gertrude was exceedingly social in her disposition, rejoiced in a numerous circle of friends, and was not in the least stuck up.

There was a large Thomas cat—an enormous creature—that often came to call upon Gertrude, in a friendly way, and spend a sociable evening. Silver-gray along the back, annular stripes on the tail, white feet, snow-white breast, large, lustrous, prominent eyes, and a magnificent pair of *whiskers*; in short, this Thomas cat was a splendid creature, and, as Rich thought, would afford him, if in his possession, an excellent opportunity to observe the structure of the eye. Dan, Frank Merrill, and Horace Williams, did their best to take the creature, dead or alive, but in vain.

A door opened from the wood-shed into the stable, and a passage was left to this door in piling the wood that was tiered up on either side to the height of five, and on one side seven, feet. Several times the boys had got the Thomas cat in this passage; but the wily creature either went over the top of the wood, or ran through a small hole beside the door, that it would seem no cat *could* get through. Rich nailed the mouth of a meal-bag to this hole on the stable side, and placed a board on the other, ready to put up to prevent the cat's return.

One Wednesday Horace Williams came over to spend the afternoon and take tea with Dan. Just before the tea hour, Dan, coming in, whispered to Rich, "The cat's in the passage. I can see his eyes shine just like balls of fire." Armed with sticks of wood, they approached the end of the passage, gave a fearful howl and let the wood fly; the globes of fire vanished, and they knew by the sound the cat had not gone over the wood-pile.

"He's in the bag, I know," said Dan. "I heard him squeeze through the hole. O, crimini!" and he ran to put up the piece of board. Rich and Horace lost no time in putting a string round the bag in which the cat was struggling, tearing it from the hole, and immersing it in a tub of water. Just as the struggling ceased the bell rang for supper, and flinging the bag and its contents into a horse-stall to drip and dry, they sat down to eat.

Dan sat on his mother's right hand, next to him Horace, and on her left was Gertrude's high chair; but it was empty.

"Where can Gertrude be?" said Mrs. Clemens, after pouring out the tea; "for seven years she has never before been absent from my side at meals unless sick."

A fearful suspicion crossed the mind of Rich, and catching the eye of Dan, he saw that he was similarly affected.

Hastening to the stable when the meal was over, with a light, they turned out the contents of the bag, and lo! it was poor Gertrude, that in the dark they had mistaken for the Thomas cat and drowned. Rich was very much distressed; so was Dan, as, aside from his sorrow for his mother, the cat was a favorite pet of his, and had grown up with him.

Placing the dead body of Gertrude upon the dissecting table, they locked the door for consultation. At first they thought of owning up, but finally concluded to keep the secret, and, as long as she was dead, thought they might as well make the remains of some advantage to science. Richardson possessed already one skeleton of a cat, and only cared for the eyes. Dan therefore persuaded him to mount Gertrude for him. This Rich did, making a small incision, turning the body through it, and replacing the skull and leg bones, after removing the brains and flesh, supplying the rest of the skeleton, so far as was needed, with wire.

Having already mounted several birds for Dan, he made a tree, put the birds in the branches, and having furnished Gertrude with eyes of colored glass, placed her under the tree in a natural attitude, as though watching a squirrel, the wire in the limbs enabling him to bend them in any direction. A red squirrel was also placed half way up the tree, as though alarmed by the cat. Dan was delighted, and thought he had much rather have his pet dead than alive.

All these operations were performed with closed doors, and the birds and animals placed under lock and key in the closet.

Mrs. Clemens mourned for her cat, and refused to be comforted. Gertrude's empty chair was always placed beside her; at table she often recounted the virtues of the departed, considered and spoke of the event as one of those mysterious dispensations of Providence, to which, though we cannot fathom, it is our duty to submit.

"I do wish my mother would bury that cat," said Dan. "I'm sick and tired of hearing about her—should think she might pick up another kitten."

Month after month passed, and still Mrs. Clemens mourned the loss of her pet. At the expiration of this period, Fred Evans, a cousin of Dan, came to visit him. One afternoon Dan persuaded Rich to put all the things on the table, make a grand show, and let Fred see them. To this Rich consented; the door was locked, and Fred sworn to secrecy.

On the table was placed the tree set in a block, with birds in its branches; half way up the trunk a red squirrel looking down and chattering at the cat, crouched at the roots as in act to spring.

Disposed around the tree that occupied the centre were the skeletons of various animals, wired together, and in an upright position, fastened to blocks—rabbits, dogs, a cat, wood-chuck, rooster, and pig. The tree was formed with great ingenuity, by placing a real branch in a thick block of pine, carving the spur roots from the substance of the block, and covering with moss, dried leaves, and twigs, confined with glue, while Gertrude, seated on the moss, seemed actually alive.

Horace Williams was invited, being already in the secret, to help entertain Fred, and as an intimate friend of Dan.

Rich wanted a shingle to put under one leg of the table, the floor being uneven, and sent Horace after it, who forgot to lock the door at his return.

Mrs. Clemens, having occasion for Dan, and not finding him in the house or yard, sought him in the harness-room, where she knew he spent much of his leisure time.

Opening the door upon the startled group, the first object that arrested her attention was the long lost and bitterly lamented Gertrude, as she verily thought, alive, and in the act of springing upon a squirrel. Exclaiming, "Gertrude! *my* Gertrude! where have you been?" she clasped the effigy to her breast. Alas! there was no answering caress; there was no "speculation" in those eyes of stained glass, and the dried skin rattled in her fond embrace. It was a *stuffed* cat. "What does this mean?" she cried, permitting the imposture to drop on the floor, thoroughly overcome and faint with this sudden blasting of new-born hopes. She would have fallen to the floor; but Rich and Dan conveyed her to the house, where, after seeing her safely placed in the easy-chair, Rich took to flight, feeling that *Dan* could settle the affair far better than himself.

"GERTRUDE! MY GERTRUDE!" Page 190.

It required all Dan's eloquence and power of argument to convince his mother that Gertrude was killed by mistake.

"But why did you not tell me at once, Daniel, that I might have had her properly interred, instead of making an exhibition of the remains?"

Dan at length convinced his mother that it was his affection for Gertrude that led him to take this method of keeping her in remembrance. But never after this did Mrs. Clemens deem Rich unfitted for his profession by over-sensitiveness.

CHAPTER XVII.
THE YOUNG SAMARITANS.

Richardson, who had thus far performed his operations upon animals with a common pocket-knife, a carpenter's fine saw, and some instruments he made in the shop of the village blacksmith,—making sleight of hand and mechanical skill supply the place of suitable tools,—was now able to purchase a pocket case of surgical instruments, that economized time, and greatly facilitated his labors. They were also of a better pattern than those he at times borrowed of the doctor.

Instead of going home in the vacations, he devoted the leisure afforded by the close of the academy to medical studies and experiments.

"Mr. Richardson," said the doctor, one day, after they had been enjoying a sing together, "it seems strange to me that you are not more inclined to go with me to visit patients. It is the very thing you need, especially when bones are to be set, or dislocations reduced. It is only occasionally that you go."

"Indeed, doctor, I hope you will not feel that I do not appreciate your kindness in so often inviting me, or that I am not sensible of the benefit to be thus obtained; but I look at it in this light, which perhaps is not the right one. I am young enough, and do not intend to commence practice till thoroughly fitted; and it seems to me there can be no correct practice without a thorough knowledge of first principles, and that the practice should be based upon, and grow out of, that knowledge.

"I have therefore resolved that I would, while here, endeavor to attain a knowledge of principles; operating, as I go along, on animals; going with you occasionally; economizing my means; and by and by attend lectures at Brunswick, or some place where I shall have ample opportunity for dissection, or go somewhere for hospital practice."

"I think you are correct there; but still I feel that you might, without neglecting your studies, obtain a great deal more practical knowledge as you go along, and that it would be time excellently well spent; for the human body, and not that of the animal, is the one you will have to deal with, and all you can learn from the brute will be only an approach, require to be modified a great deal, and much of it won't apply in actual practice."

"I have not the least doubt, doctor, but the course you advise is the best, but in my circumstances I cannot avail myself of it.

"Perhaps it would come with a better grace from some one else, but the people in this town have expressed great attachment to me, and estimate me far above my deserts. Now, if I should go much with you to visit patients, bleed, and pull teeth, and reduce dislocations, as you would have me, every academy scholar who wanted a tooth pulled, or a gum-boil lanced, would be running to me, because they would think I should not hurt them so much as you.

"People who wanted a sore opened, others, who are personally attached to me, would come for slight complaints. Many persons who are ashamed to send for you, because they owe you, would think, 'Perhaps Mr. Richardson will do just as well; he's been studying a good while with the doctor.' And thus all my time would be frittered away, and nothing to show for it."

The doctor broke into a hearty laugh, and said, "I will yield the point, Mr. Richardson. I must acknowledge you have made out a strong case."

"That is the way I look at it. I am wheeling two wheelbarrows now,—studying medicine, and teaching,—and I don't mean to wheel three."

At the close of a long, hot day, the latter part of May, Clement Richardson and his brother, wearied with toil, were seated, one on the anvil, the other on the forge.

Somewhat more than a year had passed since their misfortune. During that period their condition had very much improved, owing to the following circumstance. Cast steel had been introduced, but only a few smiths in the country were able to use it.

More care and judgment were required in working it than the old material, and the aid of borax was necessary to weld it with iron. The old smiths around Richardson would have nothing to do with "the new-fangled stuff," stuck to blistered steel and a sand weld.

But Clement Richardson belonged to a race ever open to new ideas, and perceived at a glance the value of the new metal. He had seen his father use borax to braze the threads of his vice, as also saw plates, and soon learned to use the steel, and consequently monopolized all the work in his vicinity. For there is no comparison between blistered and cast steel for an edge tool.

Their business, however, received a still greater impulse about a month before the period to which we refer. There had been little improvement in farming tools in that vicinity; the old iron pitch and manure forks were everywhere used. Clement Richardson went to Massachusetts to buy steel and iron, and there saw a patent spring steel pitchfork. He came home, and made forks with an improvement that did not infringe on the patent, and the operation proved very profitable.

"Clem," said Robert, "our year during which we were to have this shop free will soon be out. What say you for buying the old homestead back? We can pay a few hundred down, give a mortgage back, and what we should pay for rent will go towards shrinking the debt."

"The rent of the shop won't be much, Robert, and you know we were to have the rent of the house free from the time of occupancy. Suppose we wait till then."

"What if Montague should sell it over our heads?"

"I'll speak to him, and get the refusal of it."

When the brothers got home, they found a letter from Rich, containing a portion of his hard earnings, that he had sent to aid his parents. His father, however, sent the money back, informing Rich of the success of the new forks, and telling him they were getting money much faster than he was.

Waiting till his wages for the next term fell due, Rich expended the whole in the purchase of books more modern than those found in the collection of his patron, and containing principles the latter would by no means have approved.

Rich was seated in his room, earnestly engaged in study, when he was roused by a great rumpus on the stairs. In a moment the door was flung violently open, and Dan and Frank Merrill rushed into the room.

Dan had evidently been crying, for the tears stood in his eyes then, and Frank was not far from it.

"Excuse us, Mr. Richardson, for coming in so, but—"

"But you couldn't help it. What is the matter?"

"O, Mr. Richardson, don't you think! Frank, and Horace, and me were going down to the river, to go in swimming, and there was Ned Baker, Clinton Blanchard, and a whole lot of boys, had got his dog Rover, the prettiest dog you ever did see, and they'd got a rope round his neck, and were going to drown him."

"What were they going to drown him for?"

"Because they were at play with him, and pushed him under a cart; the wheel went over his hind leg, and ground it all up."

"You don't know how pitiful he looked, Mr. Richardson," said Merrill; "there they were, dragging him along on three legs, his broken leg hanging down, and he whining enough to break your heart. I never will like Clin Blanchard after this, to treat his dog so, that he pretended to love so much! I think it's real mean."

"So we got 'em to give him to us," said Dan; "and we've brought him to you, Mr. Richardson, for you to doctor him, and make him well. Will you, Mr. Richardson? Don't kill him. O, don't, please don't. You won't kill him; will you?"

And Dan, who was as noble-hearted a boy as the sun ever shone upon, could hold in no longer, and burst into tears.

"I am not so bloodthirsty as you may suppose," said Rich, half offended at the implied distrust.

"I didn't mean that, Mr. Richardson. We all love you, and know you are just as kind and good as can be. But—"

"But you know I like to experiment upon animals. Well, I'll do all I can for Rover, just as though he was my brother. So don't cry any more. Where is he?"

"Horace has got him at the door."

Rover indeed presented a sorry sight. His tongue was hanging out of his mouth, the broken leg hung dangling, covered with dust and blood. He whined piteously when any one even looked at it, appeared frightened, the water ran from his eyes, and he from time to time looked up beseechingly in the face of Horace, who held him by the collar.

"Poor fellow! he's crying," said Frank; and with his handkerchief he wiped the tears from his eyes. "I suppose his leg hurts him."

"Give him some water," said Rich.

The dog drank eagerly, and seemed revived.

"Now give him something to eat."

He ate but sparingly, and, evidently feeling assured, wagged his tail in acknowledgment.

"See how grateful he is," said Horace.

"He knows he's among friends," replied Rich.

"Better kill him at once," said Mrs. Clemens, "and put him out of misery. He will die."

"Kill him!" howled Dan; "kill him! O, mother, I shouldn't think you would talk so. He's worth forty old cats. We're going to make him get well. What's the use of studying so much to be a doctor, if you can't help anybody?"

"Well spoken, Dan," said Rich. "Take him to the barn."

Rich cut off the leg of one of Dan's old boots, and drew it over Rover's nose, to prevent him from biting them. They placed him on the table, and strapped him down.

"Boys," he said, after examination, "this is a compound fracture. The bones of the foot are all ground up, the skin broken, and the muscles bruised, and filled with gravel. The limb can't be set; it will rot off, this warm weather, before it will heal. The only way to save him is to amputate below the hock, and save the hock joint. Which would you prefer, kill him, let him alone to die himself, or amputate, and have a dog with three legs?"

The boys were a unit in favor of amputation. He therefore, having previously instructed his young assistants in what manner to hold the arteries and the limb, took it off, and tied the blood-vessels, sponged and bound up the wound.

Dan made him a bed by putting some straw in a corner, and covering it with a horse blanket, and, cutting some wide leather straps from the old chaise boot, they fastened him in such a manner that he could not move to his own injury. Rover whined terribly during the operation, but when it was finished, and the leg bound up in cold water, he became quiet, licked Dan's fingers when he took off the muzzle, and wagged his tail, no doubt sensible that he was handled gently, and that no harm was intended.

Dan got his mother to make a pillow-case. He stuffed it with chaff, and placed the wounded leg on it to keep it up (as it was shorter than the other), and make Rover as comfortable as possible. They then patted him, told him to lie still, and leaving the stable, got their lessons together in Dan's house.

When Dan got up the next morning, he found, sitting on the door-step, a little dog. His eyes were so bright they sparkled; and his back was black, also his ears and head; there was a ring of white around his neck, and his breast, legs, and feet were white. The black was jet black, and the white as white as white could be; his tail was black, and curled up so crisp over his back that it seemed as though it would lift him up behind; looking, with his erect, sharp-pointed ears, and fine, glossy coat, as though he came right out of a bandbox.

Dan recognized him in a moment, and running to Rich, told him "that Carlo—Ned Baker's dog, who lived in the next house to Clinton Blanchard, Rover's former master—was sitting on the door-step, and he didn't believe but he had come to see Rover, for they had been great friends, always playing together, and there were never two dogs agreed as well as they."

When they went to the door, Carlo was scratching and whining at the stable door, and Rover whining within. They let him into the harness-room, when Carlo jumped on his friend's bed, licked his face, licked the stump of his leg, and smelt him all over. Rover licked Carlo's face in return, wagged his tail, and seemed delighted.

The new comer then rolled himself into a ball, and lay down at Rover's nose, shutting first one eye, and then the other, as though he would say, "I have come to spend the day, and I *mean* to."

"That is capital," said Rich. "He has come on a visit of consolation. The patient will recover a great deal faster for having him here."

The two dogs took their breakfast together, and great was the surprise of Horace and Frank when they called, on their way to school, to know how Rover did, and found Carlo nursing him.

Another boy afterwards told them, "that when he first got up in the morning, he saw Carlo running along the road, with his nose to the ground." It was evident that, missing his companion, he had scented the track, and followed on till he found him.

About the middle of the afternoon Carlo went home; but at seven o'clock the next morning he returned, accompanied by three more dogs; one a great Newfoundland—Neptune. They all went up and smelt of Rover, sat round a while, and then disappeared, one after another, Carlo remaining, as before.

"I suppose," said Dan, "he went and saw all these dogs, told them what had happened to Rover, and so they came to see him."

The patient recovered rapidly; the stump healed, the ligatures came away, and it was evident the ends of the bones were well covered. Rich permitted both the dogs to lick it, which hastened the process of healing very much. Dr. Ryan came to see it, had a hearty laugh, congratulated Rich upon his success in this maiden effort, the fine appearance of the stump, and told him "He ought to give his patient a wooden leg."

Rover was now permitted to get up. The boys washed him with soap suds, rubbed him dry, and permitted him to walk out every day, and lie in the sun, on the grass. He was a beautiful dog—a spaniel, with a fine silky coat.

Carlo frisked around, barked, lay on his back, rolled over, and expressed his joy in every imaginable way.

Rover soon began to run about the yard, and follow Dan round the premises, going (till he became tired) as well on three legs as four. One noon, Dan came home from school, and found neither of the dogs at home. He was greatly disturbed, for Rover had now become very dear to him.

"I expect," said Mrs. Clemens, "he has gone back to his old home and master."

"Mother, I don't believe Rover is such a fool as that. Go back to the fellow who was going to murder him! I know he loves me better than that."

"I guess," said Rich, "he has gone to return some of the calls that have been made on him." So it proved. For when Dan came home at night, both dogs had returned, bringing two more with them.

Mrs. Clemens gradually became attached to Rover, till at length he completely won her heart, and filled the void left by the loss of Gertrude.

The boys were apprehensive that other dogs would pick upon Rover, now that he was disabled, and no longer able to defend himself or make his escape; but it was just the reverse. He found the warmest sympathy everywhere. When, in company with other dogs, he became tired and fell behind, they would stop and wait for him to come up; and if any strange dog had imposed upon Rover, they would have torn him to pieces in a moment.

Rich made him a wooden leg, carved to match one of his own. At first he held it up altogether, but after a while would use it to stand upon, and put it down when he became tired, and walk a little; then hold it up and run. He soon found that by its aid he could jump up on Dan.

It improved his looks wonderfully, as it prevented his hip from dropping, and Dan said "that he always wanted it on when they or he had company." Rover was a water spaniel, and Dan had to take the leg off when he went into the water, as it buoyed up his hinder parts, and interfered with swimming.

CHAPTER XVIII.
DAN WANTS TO KNOW HIMSELF.

Dan Clemens had taken at the first very little interest in the peculiar studies and experiments of his teacher; indeed, they were to him, a kindly-affectionate boy, rather revolting; but after the successful operation upon Rover, his feelings underwent a complete change; he was enraptured with the skill, firmness, and tender feeling manifested by Rich, spent a great deal of time at the dissecting table, and manifested a strong desire to obtain, at least, some general knowledge in respect to the mechanism of his own frame.

One evening he was seated in the harness-room, watching Rich, who was examining the stump of Rover's leg, that had become sore from the pressure of the wooden substitute, and devising some way to remedy it, when he suddenly exclaimed,—

"Mr. Richardson, how do they cut off a man's leg?"

"Very much as I did that dog's; only they use a tourniquet to compress the vessels and stop the circulation, then cut through the flesh, saw off the bones, and put ligatures on the ends of the arteries."

"What is it makes the great difference between the arteries and the veins, so that folks say, if you cut an artery, you'll bleed to death in no time. But they never speak so about veins; it's always arteries."

"I can't explain it to you, without telling you something about the heart, to start with."

"Well, tell me. O, do tell me, please."

"You saw the hog's heart I had the other day. Do you remember how it looked?"

"It looked something like an egg little end up."

"Well, a hog's heart is very much like a man's, so that one will do to represent the other. You noticed that it was smooth, and stood out about its whole bigness clear from everything, except at the base, where it joined the body?"

"Yes, sir."

"On each side of the base are two appendages, wrinkled, and shaped like an ear, denoting cavities within called from them the auricles, and into these cavities run several tubes that connect them to the parts adjacent. They are called auricles because they look so much like an ear."

"I know what they are. I saw the butcher cut them off, when he trimmed our hog's harslet: he called them deaf ears, and said they were poison."

"The heart is a hollow muscle, that contracts and dilates with great force. It is not dependent upon the will, but operates in virtue of a natural law. Through the middle of the heart, from the base to the summit, runs a partition, leaving a chamber on each side, between which there is no direct communication: they are distinguished by the terms right and left auricles. In addition to this, there is a cross parting on each side, thus making four chambers, the two upper retaining the name of auricles, the two lower denominated ventricles.

"I will now explain to you the use of all this. The right auricle opens into the large trunk vein of the body, that, in connection with the others, brings back the blood from the extremities, after the arteries have distributed it. It has also another opening into the right ventricle below it. The auricle on the other side of the partition (the left) is pierced by four veins that enter the lungs, called pulmonary veins, and also by another passage communicates with the ventricle beneath it. Now let us talk about ventricles. The right ventricle is entered by the great pulmonary artery that carries all the blood in the body through the lungs. The left ventricle is penetrated by the great artery, called the great aorta. In each of these cross partitions, there are valves that will permit blood to pass from the auricles into the ventricles, but not to return. There are also valves at the roots of the arteries that permit the blood to go from the heart into the arteries, but not to return. There are no valves at the roots of the veins that enter the auricles, nothing to obstruct the flowing of the blood from them into the auricles. Thus the roots of the veins arise from the auricles, and the roots of the arteries from the ventricles. Do you understand this description, because it is the foundation of all that follows—understand what a valve is?"

"Yes, sir; the clapper in our pump-box is a valve; it lets the water come up out of the well into the pump, but it won't let a drop go back."

"Well said; just so the valves in the partings of the heart permit the blood to pass from the auricles into the ventricles, but not to go back; thus, also, the valves placed at the roots of the arteries permit the passage of the blood from the ventricles into the arteries, but not the return of it to the heart. Do you understand this?"

"Yes, sir."

To make it more evident, Rich drew the heart, the veins, and the arteries entering it, with chalk, and the main branches of both.

"Now let us, for the clearer perception of what you wish to know, consider the march of the blood: and we might as well begin at the heart as anywhere."

"I think I can understand it better to commence there."

"From the right ventricle of the heart, springs the pulmonary artery, which, separating into several branches, some of them not larger than hairs, carries the blood into all portions of the lungs, where they communicate with the terminations of the pulmonary veins, which, receiving the blood from the arteries, bring it back to the left auricle, uniting, as they approach the heart, into four large veins, called the pulmonary veins. From the left ventricle rises the main artery (or great aorta), which, receiving all the blood of the body poured into it by the pulmonary veins, distributes it over the trunk and limbs, branching in every direction, the divisions gradually becoming smaller and smaller as they approach the extremities: here they communicate with the extremities of the veins which bring back the blood to the right auricle. So much for the aqueducts; now we will look at the action of the force-pump itself. The heart is a hollow muscle. All the valves and division walls we have been talking about are muscular in their texture, and moved by a network of muscles and minute tendons, tough and elastic, like the gizzard of a fowl, and capable of contraction and expansion. We will suppose the right auricle to be full of blood that has been brought by the veins from the fingers, toes, the substance of the heart itself, the lungs, and the liver, and poured into it. This blood is dark-colored; called black blood. It has washed the whole body. The instant it enters the auricle, that organ contracts and forces it into the ventricle below it; the valve holds it there: then the ventricle contracts and forces it into the pulmonary artery; the valve of the artery holds it there: the auricle expands, fills, again contracts, fills the ventricle, that, in its turn, forces the blood into the artery, and thus, by successive leaps, it passes into and through the lungs, enters the pulmonary veins, and is by them brought back to the left auricle. It is now no longer black blood, but bright, red, arterial blood: before it was venous."

"What makes it red?"

"I don't know. It is supposed by being brought in contact with the air in the cells of the lungs. When the auricle receives this red blood, it contracts, forces it into the left ventricle beneath, then the ventricle in its turn contracts, forces it into the main artery, and by this and its branches it is carried to the extremities, to come back in one continual round, as long as life lasts. It *is* life; for the moment the heart ceases to contract and dilate, insensibility takes place, and death instantly follows."

"It seems to me that the left side of the heart has a great deal more work to do than the right, for the left has to force the blood into the main artery, and all over the body, to the toes, the fingers, the brain: but the right ventricle only has to force it through the lungs that are close by, touch the heart, and it is a short route."

"True, and for this reason, the muscles of the left ventricle, which force the red blood of the great circulation through the main artery, are much more numerous and stronger than those of the right, which has so much less work to perform. It is the powerful contraction of the muscles of the left ventricle, causing the point of the heart to strike the fifth or sixth rib, that creates the throb you can feel; they exert power enough to send all the blood of the body through the heart twenty-three times in an hour."

"I had no idea matters were going ahead inside of me at that rate."

"You must bear in mind that I have described these things separately, but in the order of nature, it is quite another matter. The red blood from the lungs arrives at the left, and the black blood from the veins at the right auricle at the same instant; both auricles contract at once, and force the blood into their respective ventricles; both ventricles contract together and force the blood into the arteries; and thus it goes on in a person of the feeblest pulse; these alternate motions occupy, when in a state of health, but a second; the pulse at your wrist is the throb of the artery, the stroke of the heart. What do you suppose now is the force of that stroke, when the left ventricle contracts?"

"I'm sure I don't know."

"Well, the blood has been known to spurt more than five feet from the artery of the neck (carotid) when first cut. You see, now, why it is so dangerous to wound a large artery: the blood spurts at every stroke of the heart, while in the veins there is no such pressure or direct connection; besides, as the veins are designed not to carry the blood from the heart, but to bring it back, they are also furnished with numerous valves that favor the flow of blood towards the heart, but not from it."

"There is one thing I can't understand. When a man's leg is cut off, all the arteries and veins cut, how does the blood get back to the heart when the ends of the arteries are tied, and there is no communication between them and the veins?"

"By a provision of nature, there are many minute twigs and branches given off by the arteries all along their course, scarcely observable when the circulation is in its normal state, that are connected with veins equally small; those become enlarged by pressure, and renew the connection."

"It seems to me, Mr. Richardson, that the heart is like two pumps in two wells, side by side, only one throws a bigger stream than the other, and with more force."

"Ay, Daniel; but your mother's pump bears no comparison to the heart. During the time I have been with her, the spear has worn off, the boxes have been new leathered, and the cracks in the pump that sucked air have been covered with putty and lead; but *this* pump runs eighty, and sometimes a hundred years without the pause of a second."

"Why don't the muscles of the heart get tired, just as my legs do, and want to rest?"

"They do rest, and just as long as they work; rest a second, and work a second, day and night. The other muscles are in a state of tension all day, and then rest at night."

"Well, I mean to know how I am made up, before I am much older."

CHAPTER XIX.
DAN TRAPS LARGE GAME.

The industry of Rich was something remarkable. He was well fed, his work for Mrs. Clemens gave him abundant exercise, and kept him in vigorous health, and the habit of thorough study he had performed in college enabled him to make rapid progress.

In connection with the study of text-books he had performed a great number of operations upon animals, obtained practice in the use of instruments, and now felt disposed to comply, to a certain extent, with the doctor's advice in respect to actual practice. It was not long before an opportunity offered.

Dan Clemens had the toothache, and in spite of all the remedies his mother applied,—and they were by no means few in number—laudanum, gunpowder, pepper, cloves, the stem of a pumpkin smoked in a pipe, hot salt, camphor, and new rum,—was half crazy with it.

"Mr. Richardson," said Dan, "will you please pull my tooth? I don't want to go to Dr. Ryan. I know he'll hurt me awfully."

"Nobody can pull a tooth, Daniel, without inflicting pain. They are designed to stay in—the second crop."

"But you won't hurt me as much as he will. He won't care if he does hurt me. Besides, you haven't got such an awful-looking thing to pull 'em with as his is." Rich had purchased, with his other instruments, forceps of a modern pattern, while the doctor used the huge old corkscrew instruments. "Do, please, Mr. Richardson. I won't tell anybody; so you won't have your time taken up by boys running to you."

Rich put the instrument on the tooth Dan indicated, and took it out in a moment. Dan gave a fearful yell, and ran to the fire-place.

"I told you it would hurt you."

"I don't care. Dr. Ryan would have hurt me more."

Notwithstanding Dan's promise of secrecy, it got wind somehow, and Rich soon had considerable practice of that kind. But, as he had now made good progress in study, and the money was very acceptable, he became reconciled to it.

An opportunity was soon after this presented that Rich did not fail to improve. The people of the neighborhood were engaged in hauling a barn, and a young man, in attempting to fling a skid under the building while in motion, received a compound fracture of the thigh. Dr. Ryan was called. He sent for Dr. Slaughter, and took Rich with him, who required no solicitation, as it was the first opportunity he had enjoyed of witnessing an important operation.

The limb was taken off some distance above the knee, leaving that joint entire, it having escaped injury by being pressed into the mud. Weary of dissecting animals, Rich longed to obtain this limb. There it lay, a well-developed leg and part of the thigh of a young man. He took it in his hands after the operation was performed, and gloated over it as an antiquarian over a rare coin. His fingers itched, and he felt an intense desire to possess it.

"Dr. Ryan," he whispered, "won't you ask for this leg, and then give it to me?"

"It would be of no use, Mr. Richardson; they would think the leg must be buried, or the man would not do well. It would cost me my practice. They are that superstitious. But if I were you, I would find out where they bury it, and dig it up to-night."

The doctor took up the limb, and carrying it into the kitchen, said, "This leg must be put in a box and buried."

"That it must," replied the father of the young man; "for I've heard say, ever since I can remember, if a dog or any critter got hold of any part of a person what had been cut off, that person would feel it just as though the limb was still on."

"I'll make the box, and help bury it," said Rich.

"I should be much obliged if you would, Mr. Richardson. Neighbor Pollard, here, will help you. Where ought it to be buried, doctor?"

"In the graveyard with his relatives, to be sure. It is part of a Christian, and the rest of him will go to keep it company some time."

A daughter of the family had died some years before, and Pollard proposed that the leg should be buried beside her grave, which was done.

The doctor had proposed that it should be put in a box, in order to keep it clean, and in a good state for Rich to dissect, and be placed in the cemetery, because that lot was in a retired spot.

That night Rich dug up the limb, and hid it in the haymow, meaning to dissect it the next night, in order to escape the sharp eyes of Dan Clemens, and then keep the bones in the doctor's study, where there was a closet.

Rich was detained at school that afternoon by a boy who had failed to get his lesson. When he reached the house he found a man in the barn floor loading hay on a cart from the very mow in which he had concealed the leg, while Dan was on the mow pitching down the hay.

"I am so glad you have come, Mr. Richardson! Mr. Bangs wants a ton of hay, and I told Daniel he had better be doing what he could till you came."

Rich was terribly frightened. His color went and came.

"Daniel," he cried, flinging off his coat, "run into the house quick, and get me a drink; I am very thirsty."

Leaping upon the mow, he beheld one corner of the box already uncovered. Another fork full would have done the business. Before Dan returned with his water, he had put it in a safe place. There was but one window in the harness-room, and while Dan was gone after the cow, Rich nailed the horse-blanket over it, in order that no one passing might observe a light, as he intended to dissect after the family—or at least Dan, of whom he was the most apprehensive—were asleep.

Having accomplished his purpose, he was passing from the stable to the house, when Dr. Ryan, who was riding by in his gig, called to him, and said,—

"Mr. Richardson, Coolbroth is dead."

"Dead!"

"Yes; died about an hour ago. Very strange. Never was more surprised in my life. Thought he was doing well. Sank all at once. Going to be buried to-morrow forenoon. Hot weather—they can't keep him. Good night."

"Good night."

Rising from supper as soon as possible without attracting attention, Rich made the best of his way to Coolbroth's. He met Pollard there, and found the family in great affliction.

"We don't any of us know what's afore us, Mr. Richardson," said Pollard; "'cause, if we had, we might have saved ourselves the trouble o' buryin' that leg, for we've got to dig it up ag'in in the mornin'."

"What are you going to dig it up for?"

"'Cause they want to lay him in that spot, side o' his sister; and then they want to put the leg in the coffin with the rest of him, as rights they should, poor feller."

"What time to-morrow will the funeral take place?"

"Ten o'clock. I shall have to be stirring 'arly, and begin by sunrise to dig the grave, 'cause they've nobody 'cept myself to call on, and I've got a master sight to see to."

Rich inquired no further, but went home in no little perturbation. He sat up in his room till twelve o'clock, then crept down stairs in his stocking feet, with his shoes in his hand, and without a light. Since the death of Gertrude, rats had multiplied on the premises. They had a regular road from the stable, through the porch, which they entered from beneath, through a hole in the floor. The night previous to the occurrences now to be narrated, one of these vermin had gnawed his way into the flour barrel. Dan had set a steel trap at the hole in the shed, where the rats came up, and quite out of the track of any one going to the stable. But Rich, fumbling along in the dark, put his foot in it.

The trap was one of the old-fashioned rat traps, made to *kill* and *hold*, with a smart spring, and the jaws on the inside armed with teeth, like a saw.

The pain and surprise combined caused Rich to utter an involuntary scream, that, breaking on the stillness of midnight, alarmed the household.

Mrs. Clemens lay in bed, screaming alternately, "Murder," and "Thieves," at the top of her voice. Dan rushed down stairs in his night-gown, when Rich called to him, and explained matters.

By the time Dan had procured a light, Rich had drawn his foot out of the trap, and Mrs. Clemens and the hired girl made their appearance.

"Mr. Richardson," said Mrs. Clemens, "you have hurt your foot terribly. The blood is oozing through your stocking. Let me make a slippery elm poultice, and put on it."

"It is a mere scratch, Mrs. Clemens—only skin deep."

"There is some water in the tea-kettle that must be blood-warm now. Betty, bring a small tub, for Mr. Richardson to bathe his foot, and a sponge."

"There is no need of it, Mrs. Clemens. Cold water is better. I can wash it in my chamber."

The night was fast spending. It would be daylight by the time he reached the cemetery. Rich had no time to spare, and wished Mrs. Clemens was in another hemisphere.

"At least, Mr. Richardson, let me get you some bandages, and some new rum and wormwood, to bathe it in. Daniel will take the things up stairs."

"Indeed, Mrs. Clemens, I thank you very much; but I have some sticking-plaster in my chamber."

And Rich, hastily bidding them good night, went to his room.

When there, he found that the jaws of the trap had cut deeper than he supposed, and the wound began to be stiff and painful. He bound it up, and taking an old boot, cut out the vamp, and was by this means enabled to wear it.

"What shall I do?" said Rich to himself. "I ought to be at the graveyard *now*. It will be two hours before that old lady will go to sleep, and I never can get out of the house without her knowledge."

Rich's room was in the second story of the L, and the water-spout ran near the window. After waiting half an hour, and finding all was still, Rich, raising the sash as gently as possible, descended by the conductor to the ground, and taking the box from the barn, went limping along in the bright moonlight, the box under one arm, and a shovel in the other hand. The jaws of the trap had bruised the numerous tendons that run along the top of the foot, and every step was a pang.

"I wish I had never seen this confounded leg," said Rich. "If I can only get it where it came from, it's the last thing I'll ever dig up."

CHAPTER XX.
GOES FOR WOOL, AND GETS SHORN.

The graveyard to which Rich now directed his steps was the original burying-place of the town; but another having been provided, in a more central location, it had been little used for years, and was overgrown with bushes and sweet fern, an occasional spruce or hemlock assuming almost the dimensions of a tree.

Narrow, in proportion to its breadth, one end of the lot approached the main road, the intervening space being level, and clear of obstructions, except near the gate, where the wall was fringed with spruce, sumach, and hazel bushes, a very dense clump of spruce and dwarf birch growing just beside the main entrance.

Notwithstanding the lonely situation and neglected aspect of the place, there were many very handsome monuments scattered over its surface. But the hands that reared them were mouldering in the dust, and their descendants, becoming interested in the new cemetery, the ancient graveyard seemed likely to return to its original state of forest, and that indeed at no distant period, being already enclosed on three sides by a growth of majestic pines, whose roots, in several places, had flung down the wall. A few rods beyond the main entrance, the road, making a sharp turn, led up a hill.

Far removed from any habitation or sound of busy life, this resting-place of the departed lay reposing in the clear moonlight that seemed to embrace it, silvering with its wavy light the rough walls, the monuments of the dead, and the foliage, bathed in dew. So deep was the stillness, that the slow and painful tread of Rich on the hard-beaten road was distinctly audible.

He was about half way from the road to the gate, when all at once rang out with startling effect upon the still air,—

"Come here to me. What are you hangin' off there for, old Bright? Come here to me, or I'll put the cold iron into your liver."

The next moment his ears were greeted with that peculiar slat and jingle that ensues when the tongue cattle on the top of a hill throw up their heads in order to hold back a heavy load.

"Good heavens!" thought Rich; "I am beset indeed. It is Sam Waterhouse, with his four-ox team."

Regardless of his lame foot, he crept into the bunch of bushes near the gate, with the box and shovel. In a few moments a large dog came up the hill, followed by Sam, who stopped his cattle opposite the gate, to let them breathe. The dog, in the mean time running along the road, came upon

Richardson's track, and following it up to the bushes, began to bark furiously. Fearing discovery, Rich crept along through the scattering bushes, into the thicker growth, still proceeding in a line parallel with the main road, and not far from it. The dog, however, continued to follow, barking so furiously, that Rich, afraid that Waterhouse would come to see what the dog was barking at, stepped out into the road without attracting the notice of Sam, till he was within a few feet of him, who, supposing him to have come by the road from the village, exclaimed,—

"Good evenin', Mr. Richardson; or, ruther, mornin'; for I reckon it's mighty near daybreak. I was jest thinkin' of goin' ter see what the dog was barkin' at; thought may be 'twas a coon; they're apt to be out these moonlight nights; but I s'pose 'twas you he hearn. Didn't 'spect ter run foul o' you, this time in the mornin'. S'pose you had a sudden call. Doctors and teamsters, they must kalkerlate to be broke o' their rest, and folks say you're gettin' ter be quite a doctor, and Dr. Ryan speaks master well o' you."

"Sick and dying time, Mr. Waterhouse," said Rich, wishing to turn the conversation from himself, and not heeding the question of the other; "I wonder you should be going away with a team when young Coolbroth is to be buried to-morrow."

"Wouldn't have gone for anything. 'Tain't to save money, nor 'arn money, but I'd 'greed to deliver these ere shooks, and was 'bleeged ter. Seems to me you limp. I can't see quite so well as I used ter, 'specially in the night, but I thought you favored that left foot somewhat."

"Yes; I have a sore foot."

"Jammed it? Jammed the nail off? 'Cause, if ye have, there's nothin' so good to take the soreness out as mullein leaves, steeped in new rum."

"I stepped into a rat trap in the dark."

"My songs! that's dreadful bad. Might give you the lockjaw. There's nothin' 'll take that ere iron rust out o' the flesh like the marrer (marrow) of a hog's jaw."

"I don't doubt it," said Rich, to whom this prosing was perfect agony; "but I must go on."

"So must I. Back, Bright! Her, Buck, up! Stan' up there, old Star."

Rich made as though he would have gone on, and soon enjoyed the satisfaction of hearing the sound of Sam's wheels die away in the distance; but when he again recovered his box and shovel, the gray light was streaking the eastern sky.

Flinging off both coat and vest, he strained every nerve to dig a hole in which to deposit the box at the same depth, and in the same place as before. In momentary expectation of seeing Pollard arrive, he exerted himself till the sweat trickled down his cheeks, for, whenever he stopped to take breath, the early birds were singing in the trees around him.

He had scarcely time to deposit the last shovelful, and congratulate himself upon his success, when the sound of wheels was heard rapidly approaching, and Pollard, accompanied by another person, drove up to the graveyard gate.

IN THE GRAVEYARD. Page 226.

Crouching behind tombstones and bushes, he crept on his hands and knees to the back wall, and not daring to clamber over for fear of being seen, pushed out the stones, and made his way through the gap into the woods, as Pollard and his assistant reached the spot he had just left.

Hiding his shovel in the woods, not daring to take it, lest he should meet some early riser, Rich, in pain and perturbation, limped through fields and pastures, till he at length, to his great delight and relief, reached his boarding-place.

But his troubles were not ended. Every door was fastened. He could not, with his lame foot, and entirely exhausted, clamber up the spout to his room, and Rover began to bark in the porch, where he slept, with a violence that Rich knew would soon awaken the whole family.

Mrs. Clemens was very particular—extremely so—in respect to fastening the doors at night, and there was no outbuilding to which Rich could obtain access except the pig-sty. That was merely buttoned on the outside. But this was too far from the house to suit his purpose, and moreover, exposed to the observation of Dan, while milking, who was always the first one up in the house.

Dan was full of energy. His custom was to wake early, go directly to the barn-yard, milk, bring the milk in, call the girl to strain it, and then start off with the cows to pasture, returning by breakfast time. Rich was familiar with the habits of Dan, and while deliberating with respect to some place of concealment, was startled by hearing him shove back the bolt of the end door. Close to the steps grew a large lilac bush, and near that was a pile of apple-tree brush that had been hauled out of the orchard. Rich ran behind the pile, and crouched to the ground, watching Dan as he came out, rubbing his eyes, and the moment he saw him sit down to a cow, crawled through the lilac bush, and stole quietly to his room. Pulling off the boot, he washed the gravel and dust from his foot, flung himself upon the bed, and sank into a slumber so profound that Dan, unable to arouse his teacher, at breakfast time, by knocking on the door, was compelled to enter, and shake him.

It seemed, indeed, as though the complications connected with this fruitless undertaking were never to have an end. Scarcely were they seated at the breakfast table, when Mrs. Clemens observed—

"Mr. Richardson, you look pale and worn out. I fear you passed a sleepless night. Daniel said you were lying on the outside of the bed, with your clothes on, when he went to call you. Will you not have an alum curd on your foot this morning? It is so cleansing."

"I think there is no need, Mrs. Clemens. A bruise in that place must be more or less painful for a time. I slept very soundly indeed this morning."

"Well, I shall insist upon Daniel's taking you to school with the horse. He is in the barn."

"You are very kind, and I shall esteem it a great favor; and if you please I will take a luncheon, and Daniel can bring me back at night; for I scarcely feel equal to the walk."

No sooner was this offer disposed of than Dan said,—

"Mother, did you hear anybody prowling round the house last night?"

"No, my dear: why do you ask?"

"Because the shovel is gone; somebody must have stole it."

"Perhaps it is mislaid."

"No, it ain't; I have looked everywhere. I wanted it to clean the barn."

"I heard Rover barking dreadfully this morning; it waked me up. Did you hear anybody round the house, Mr. Richardson? Being kept awake by your wound, you would be more likely to hear any strange noise."

"Well, Mrs. Clemens,—ahem!—indeed, I think there was some one went out of the yard last night."

"That's it, mother; and that's who Rover was barking at."

"But how could they get into the barn?"

"They might have a key, and unlock the padlock. Most anything will unlock a padlock. But you must get another shovel, mother."

"We will wait awhile. It may come to light,—might get into that load of hay I sold,—be pitched up out of the floor with the hay. Mr. Richardson, your face seems flushed; does your foot pain you?"

"No, ma'am; it is quite easy now."

The excessive soreness of Richardson's foot was occasioned by his use, or rather abuse of it. But it recovered rapidly as soon as he began to afford it rest, and make the proper applications. After enjoying a good night's sleep, he told Mrs. Clemens he would like the loan of the horse, to ride over to the next town after school at night, call on Perk, and return in the evening. The next morning, when Dan went to feed the pigs, the shovel was lying in the pig's bed, half covered in straw.

"I told you it would come to light, Daniel. You used it to clean the pig-pen, and left it there. The pigs threw it down, and rooted the straw over it."

"I didn't, mother. Haven't cleaned the pig-pen. Mr. Richardson does that; I am afraid of the pigs. Somebody stole it, and brought it back."

"Borrowed it, you mean, my dear. You should never make such accusations."

Dr. Ryan laughed till the tears ran down his cheeks when, some time afterwards, Rich told him the result of his efforts to obtain the leg.

"It is the first time I ever attempted anything of the kind," said Rich; "it shall be the last. I'll stick to dogs, cats, and rabbits till I have money to procure what I need."

CHAPTER XXI.
PROGRESS AND PREJUDICE.

There was a mystery connected with Richardson's lameness that the village gossips could never fathom. He was too important a personage to escape comment. It was well known that he was so lame as to be compelled to ride to school on three consecutive days; and yet Sam Waterhouse declared he met him and talked with him at the old graveyard at three o'clock on the morning he put his foot in the trap, and that he did not appear to be much lame. Sam, however, was in the habit of drinking too freely of New England rum, and always took a jug with him when on the road; thus the majority, after a while, concluded Waterhouse had made too free with the contents of his jug, and imagined it all.

Rich, after this, assisted in several important operations in which the two doctors were engaged. He likewise, when he could do it and not interfere with his school, opened sores, administered medicines, let blood, and dressed wounds, at the request of Dr. Ryan, who lost no opportunity of bringing him forward, and became more and more attached to him every day.

When bones were to be set, Dr. Ryan, if the fracture was in any respect a bad one, sent for Dr. Slaughter; but, as his own practice was large, often relinquished the subsequent care of the fracture to Rich, and paid him for it. In this manner, and by rigid economy, he was enabled to lay by a considerable sum, besides purchasing some necessary instruments and books.

The good doctor was well aware that whenever he left the care of a patient to Rich, whether it was a case of disease, or a wound, or broken bone, that he practised a treatment quite different from the established method; but as the patients generally did well, he made no troublesome inquiries, and even turned a deaf ear to the hints of Dr. Slaughter in respect to innovations upon the good old substantial practice.

It was very hot weather, the middle of August, and a lad of seventeen received a terrible cut in his thigh, by coming too near his father while he was mowing oats. Dr. Ryan was away from home, attending the funeral of a near relative in a distant town; the family instantly sent for Rich. The wound, fortunately, was worse in appearance than reality, as no artery was severed, though the gash presented a most formidable appearance to inexperienced persons, and the parents were very much alarmed.

Rich quieted their fears, stopped the bleeding, cleansed, bound up, and dressed the wound. It was several days before the doctor returned. The first time he rode out to visit his patients, he encountered on the road an old acquaintance, but by no means a favorite of his, Miss Nelly Buckminster. Miss Nelly was a spinster, lived by herself in a small house left to her by her parents, and gained a livelihood by taking in spinning, weaving, and plain sewing; occasionally kept house for anybody who could endure her tongue, for she was an inveterate talker, and held very decided opinions upon all subjects. In other respects she was an excellent housekeeper, neat, industrious, economical, and an excellent cook.

Miss Nelly was very religious, exceedingly so; but her piety was of the vociferous, rather than of the introspective cast. She was the recipient of many presents. Some gave her because they thought her a very good though rather peculiar woman, some because they were afraid of her tongue, others because they knew she would tell of it from Dan to Beersheba. We think it must have been the reasons assigned that influenced so many persons to make presents to Nelly, because there was not the least satisfaction to be derived from the act itself, as Nelly, in expressing her gratitude and sense of obligation—which she never failed to do—always ignored second causes, and paid her respects to the Most High.

This might have been—undoubtedly was—good theology, but it was of the nutmeg-grater variety, and altogether corrosive in both quality and operation; for when persons bestow gifts, influenced by the purest motives, some manifestation of gratitude is pleasant, and generally expected; but no person ever received any from Nelly; her gratitude was ever directed over the heads of the *instrumentalities* to the *efficient* cause, which was not merely sound doctrine and *conservative*, but did away at once with all troublesome sense of obligation or return in kind.

Squire Dresser once sent her by the hand of his son a bushel of Indian meal. Henry knocked at the door, and gave her the bag of meal, saying,—

"Miss Buckminster, here is a bushel of flour my father sent you, and he'll call some time when he's going by to mill, and get the bag."

"No thanks to Squire Dresser; thanks to the Lord; 'twas the Lord sent it, and not the squire."

Henry had made the interview as brief as possible, in order to escape an exhortation on the subject of personal piety, that Nelly was in the habit of administering to him whenever he came to her house of an errand, and which altogether failed of producing any good impression, because he did not like her, and by reason of the snappish way in which she flung it at him.

Finding he had in his haste made a mistake, he went back and said,—

"Miss Buckminster, I made a mistake. 'Tis Indian and not wheat meal that father sent you."

"*Indian!* I should like to know what he sent *Indian* for!"

This curt reply made a good deal of sport among the neighbors.

"I don't believe the *Lord* will send her anything again very soon," said Squire Dresser.

"The old proverb is, 'Never look a gift horse in the mouth;' but she presumes to find fault with the gifts of the Lord, tells what *he* should send and what not."

Dr. Ryan, who dearly loved good living, tempted by her unrivalled skill as a cook, and confiding in his good temper and the soundness of his nerves, once employed Nelly to keep house for him. She was possessed of a very vivid imagination, and in the habit of cautioning people against doing things they never entertained the thought of doing.

It was cold, sharp weather, and the doctor had a small dog that was very fond of stretching out on the hearth before the andirons. One day the doctor came in, chilled from a long ride and stood warming himself; the dog lay stretched at full length between him and the fire.

"There! you'll kick that dog into the fire—I know you will!" screamed Nelly.

"So I will, then," said the doctor, and kicked him under the forestick.

Nelly never cautioned the doctor any more.

In some respects it was difficult to reconcile her professions with her practice: for instance, she always said in the prayer-meeting that it was a great cross for her to rise and speak; whereas it was the settled opinion of all who knew her that it would be a much greater cross for her to hold her tongue, and Captain Motley said,—

"If you nailed her down to the bench with ten-penny nails, she'd rise and take it up with her."

She always disliked people whom everybody else loved and respected, called it *man-worship*, therefore didn't like Rich, couldn't bear him. Dr. Ryan said, it was a good thing for Richardson; he ought to have one ill-wisher, to take the curse off.

"Doctor, good mornin'."

"Good morning, Nelly."

"Doctor, you never should ought to step your two feet out of this village. Dreadful works, dreadful, since you've been away. Doctor, what do you think this wicked world is comin' to? Errors in doctrine, new lights rampaging round, turnin' things upside down; errors in doctorin,' as though folks couldn't die fast enough themselves. Destruction to soul and body both."

"I expect it is coming to an end, Nelly."

"When, doctor? Any ways soon? 'Cause we ought to be on our watch guards, a girdin' up our loins and preparin'."

"O, no; I guess 'twill outlast you and me, and a good many other people. But what is the trouble now?"

"Trouble enough. Do you know, David Ryan, what a viper yer a nourishin' in yer buzom? Do you know it, David Ryan? 'Cause if you don't, it's high time you did. Do you know what that young snipper-snapper of a Richardson is, that's allowed for to lead the singin' in the Lord's house? The gals is all taken with his good looks, and the men with his 'ily tongue. But I tell you he's a—"

Here Nelly thrust her tongue into her cheek, and looked unutterable things.

"I know he's a young man of true piety, most affectionate disposition, and remarkable ability, and I won't hear a word said against him by you or anybody else."

"Jist like Deacon Starkweather; he's deceived yer both, pulled the wool over both yer eyes. I tell you he's a—"

"A what? Come, out with it. I don't like this stabbing in the dark. Speak out."

"He's a *new light*, a pestilent, pizen, *new light*," shouted Nelly, with an emphasis she expected would throw the doctor from his horse. But he stood the shock unmoved, and merely laughed.

"It's no laughin' matter. There's John Tukey's boy cut hisself awful with a scythe, and that snipper-snapper, don't you think, did it up in *cold water*, nothin' else, instead of wrappin' it up in new rum, or rum and wormwood, or salve, as you would have done, and keepin' it warm. Enough to make him ketch his death a cold!"

"Is he not doing well enough?"

"Doin' well enough! The awfullest sight of *proud* flesh; it was a sight to behold. I was there when old Granma'am Tyler put on her specs and looked at it. She exclaimed right out. Says she, 'That wound will never heal in this varsal world, with all that ere *proud* flesh in it, Matilda,' says she (that's the boy's mother). 'Let me put on some burnt alum, to eat out that proud flesh.' Matilda made answer, 'I should like to have you, granma'am.' Then the boy up and says, 'No, she shan't.' 'Some red precipitate, then, dear, and hog's lard.' No, he wouldn't have that. 'Some spruce gum, then.' No, he wouldn't have anything; nobody should consarn with it or touch it but Mr. Richardson; he knew more than Granny Tyler and all the old women in town."

"I rather think the boy was right."

"Right! That little *snipper-snapper*, that brought an ungodly *fiddle* into the *sanctuary* on the *Lord's* day, know more'n *Granny Tyler*, an experienced woman in sickness, and that's brought up a large family of children! What do you s'pose he said when he came the next day, and Matilda told him what Granny Tyler said? He jist laughed, and said all the proud flesh there was wouldn't hinder it from healing. Much he knows, to say proud flesh wouldn't hinder a cut from healing! Them's the very identical words he used. I'll stan' to it till my *dyin' day*."

"I have not the least doubt he said so."

"Well, then, doctor, I hope you'll go right in there, and put things to rights, 'cause the old folks'll hear to you, and the boy'll hear to you; and if you don't, perhaps the proud flesh'll grow worser and mortify; 'cause granny said a sore never would heal as long's there was one mite of proud flesh in it; and if the boy should die, you'll be 'countable, sartainly."

"I can't go in; I've a long ride to another part of the town before me."

"Well, you'll see, mark my word for it, there'll be trouble grow out of this."

The doctor had lost, in the course of his practice, several patients from gangrene occasioned by the load of poultices, ointments, and bandages it was then customary to apply, and he had some suspicions whether there might not be some mistake in the old practice, and resolved to permit Rich to manage matters as he thought best, having so much confidence in his judgment and discretion that he felt sure he would come to him for advice and consultation if the wound was manifesting any unfavorable symptoms.

We have no doubt our young readers share to the full the confidence of the doctor in both the ability and discretion of Rich; still it seems as though it were well to say a few words in his behalf, and in explanation.

Clean cuts, when the two sides of the wound can be brought together directly, sometimes heal without any inflammation or suppuration; as it were, stick right together. But when the parts cannot be brought together at once, and are exposed to the external air, even if bandaged, there will be inflammation, and then the wound heals by a natural process, called by physicians "granulation."

It was thus in the present instance. The boy and his father had taken a field of oats to mow and harvest, a long distance from home, and the wound had been some time exposed to the air, and by reason of the part of the body in which it was situated could not be brought together so closely as to cause it thus to heal by what surgeons call the "first intention," and adhesive inflammation occurred, as is always the case when wounded surfaces are not brought in contact at once.

The process is this. In consequence of the inflammation which then takes place, a yellow jelly-like substance is effused, covering the surfaces of the wound, called fibrin; veins and arteries from the sound flesh shoot into this, it becomes organized, another layer is thrown out, which in its turn passes through the same process; but now begins another step in the progress. From this organized fibrin spring innumerable little pointed cones, similar to the kernels of rice corn, at first of a pale red, becoming more florid as they increase in age, into which arteries and veins thrust themselves. These are the granulations. They have nerves and blood-vessels, are therefore alive, and when healthy, sensitive; and they likewise possess a disposition to unite, and when the two surfaces of a wound covered with granulations come in contact, the blood-vessels of one penetrate the other, they amalgamate and form flesh.

As they increase they contract, thus both filling the cavity and drawing the lips of the wound together, till, when it heals, the scar occupies much less space than the original cut. This process takes place when the granulations are healthy, and almost, but not completely, fill the wound, being a grain lower than the surface of the skin, and manifesting a disposition to glaze over.

At other times they are coarse, of large size, the points blunt, are spongy, pale, or blue, show no tendency to skin over, and puff up above the surface of the sound flesh, which swells and is inflamed. Physicians denominate these granulations fungus, it being found from experience that whenever granulations rise higher than the level of the surrounding surface they are not likely to form skin. This, among people in general, from the appearance, probably, goes by the name of *proud* flesh.

The old matrons cherished a mortal dread of proud flesh. They would put on their spectacles, look carefully at the wound, hold up both hands, and exclaim with alarm, "*Proud* flesh!" often times when only the proper amount of granulations was present, and they had numerous specifics for its removal—spruce gum, burnt alum, the ashes of oak bark, nutgalls, and red precipitate. But in their zeal to extirpate proud flesh, and, as they termed it, *do* something, they sometimes used little discrimination, and made war upon healthy material.

The particular thing that seemed to lie with the greatest weight upon the minds of the ancient dames and Miss Buckminster was, that, according to them, Rich was *doing nothing* for the poor lad. He was neither bleeding him, physicking him, putting on salves and heavy bandages, nor anything to kill the *proud* flesh. They made such a fuss that at last the boy, who had hitherto reposed the greatest confidence in his young physician, became a little *nervous*, and told Rich what the matrons said.

"My dear boy," said he, "there is very little *to* be *done*. What these good women call *proud* flesh is a *healthy* growth, the rudiments of new flesh, and without it your wound would *never* heal. It is no more in my power, or that of any other person, to heal your flesh than to make one hair white or black. Nature and time will do that. The inflammation has passed off, and the wound is healing. All that can be done is to keep the parts cool, defend them from the air, sustain your strength by a proper diet, and keep you quiet. The less you move, the faster your leg will heal; and as for bleeding, you have lost too much blood already from the cut."

The lad, after this, dismissing his anxieties, concerned himself no more about the proud flesh or the fears and prognostications of the matrons.

The patient in due time recovered, greatly to the satisfaction of Dr. Ryan. It also increased the reputation of Rich, though Miss Buckminster declared that "the boy should ought to have died of mortification or lockjaw, but the *Lord* overruled it and spared him for some good end, spite of the new-fangled doctor."

CHAPTER XXII.
SUITING MEANS TO ENDS.

The early frosts had now commenced. The glory of summer was succeeded by the maturity of autumn, and in the valleys here and there the white maples and ash began to assume their yellow and crimson hues. The diseases incident to the period of the year were prevalent, and Dr. Ryan was riding night and day.

As Richardson was passing the doctor's house on his way from school in the afternoon, the latter called to him, and said,—

"Mr. Richardson, I wish you would do me a favor. I am just about to step into my gig to visit a person taken with the bilious colic, in great distress, and a man has this moment gone from the door who wants me to go to see Mr. Jonathan Davis, who has cut off the tendon Achillis (heel-cord) with an adze; a clean cut. Can't you get on the back of the other horse, and take care of Mr. Davis?"

"Yes, sir. I'll leave my books in your office, and be right off."

"But you'll want some supper."

"I'll eat there after I get through."

Davis kept a good stock of tools, made his wheels, harrows, yokes, and other farming tools, and some for his neighbors. In working with an adze between his feet, the instrument glanced, and the corner of it severed the tendon of his left leg.

The Achillis tendon is large, and connected with a very strong muscle, as it sustains a great strain when the foot is thrown forward, and the weight of the body, perhaps with the addition of some burden on the shoulder, raised by it; and when broken or cut, the strong muscles of which it is a prolongation, cause it to contract very much.

Farmer Davis was a member of the choir, much attached to Rich; and, though he was somewhat disappointed at not seeing Dr. Ryan, his old physician, yet there was probably not a person in the town to whom Rich could have been sent upon such an errand where he would have found less of prejudice to contend with, either in respect to his youth, lack of experience, or any new-fangled notions he might have the reputation of entertaining.

"Good afternoon, Mr. Davis. I am sorry for your injury, and also that Dr. Ryan could not come. I expect you will hardly care to see so poor a substitute;

but I feared there might be some artery cut, and knew you needed prompt attention."

Farmer Davis was quite a different person from Miss Buckminster in many other respects besides gender, being a most skilful mechanic, and an intelligent, clear-headed man.

"Well, Mr. Richardson," he replied, "you know very well you're as welcome to my house as flowers in May; and as for this business of the leg, I don't believe that Dr. Ryan, who's doctored my family and my father's afore me, would have sent you if he hadn't known you was capable; and if he had, I don't believe, if you hadn't thought you knew what was to be done and how to do it, you'd have come."

"I have come to do the best I can, which is very little, as this is a case where art can do but little to assist nature; but if you feel any hesitation, say so; the horse is at the door; I'll go get Dr. Slaughter."

"Won't have him; he's no better than a *butcher*. Go ahead, Mr. Richardson. There must be a first time with every man. I believe the first pair of wheels I ever made were as good and well finished up as any I've made since, 'cause I took more pains; and I've heern old Captain Deering say that 'a green hand that's just learning to steer a vessel will oftentimes steer better'n an old sailor, 'cause the old fellow is careless; but t'other's scared to death all the time, and puts his whole soul into it.'"

After examining the wound, Rich said,—

"There are two methods of treating this injury, the old method and the new. I will explain both of them; you may then take your choice, and I will follow your directions."

"That's fair. Let's hear."

"You see all the tendons play in a sheath, which is fixed, and the tendons play back and forth in it."

"Just like a spyglass, one part shoves into the other."

"Yes. And they are all on the stretch, like a piece of rubber drawn out, and when they are cut, the contraction of the muscles draws the two ends apart. The muscles in the upper part of the leg have drawn one end of this heel-cord up into its sheath, and the muscles on the forward part of the leg, by bending the foot back, have drawn the other end down into its sheath. Now, the old method, that which Dr. Slaughter and Dr. Ryan both would pursue, is to search in the sheath, get hold of the ends of the cord, and sew them together, which in your case would involve the necessity of cutting to accomplish it."

"I understand that. Now what is the new fashion?"

"The old physicians thought a tendon could not unite unless the ends touched, and so used to sew them together. But it has been since proved by experiment that although it is well to bring the ends of the tendon as near to each other as can well be done, they will unite even if they are half an inch or an inch apart."

"How can they grow together if they don't touch?"

"A liquid substance exudes from the surrounding vessels, fills the sheath, thickens into a jelly, then becomes a callous, grows to the two ends, forms a bunch, and in time shrinks up and becomes just like the rest of the tendon."

"How did they find that out?"

"Men have broken the tendon and wouldn't have their leg cut open to stitch the ends together, but kept still, had splints put on, and the ends brought as near as possible in that way, got well, and recovered the use of the limb. If there's no need of cutting a hole in a sound leg to sew a tendon together, there's no need of sewing one when a hole is already cut, or of cutting it larger to get at it."

"That stands to reason. So go ahead. I don't see why there shouldn't be improvements in doctoring as well as in everything else. My father winnowed his grain in a half a bushel, and had to wait for the wind. I winnow mine when I get ready, and raise my own wind with the machine."

Rich bent the leg on the thigh, so as to relax the muscles in the calf of the leg as much as possible, then with his hands worked down the calf, bringing the upper end of the tendon down, and put a bandage around to confine the muscles and keep them from retracting; brought the foot forward in order to bring the lower end of the tendon up, and employed an assistant to keep it so.

In the mean time he went into Mr. Davis's shop, where he found tools, selected a sweeping piece of wood, and in a very few moments made a splint of sufficient length to extend from just below the knee to the toes, and that by its elliptical form partially filled the angle made by the foot and leg; he then padded the space between it and the flesh, fastened it to the leg and toes in such a manner as to keep the foot extended and prevent the patient from involuntarily moving the muscles. He now could feel the ends of the tendon, and ascertained, much to his satisfaction, that they were very nearly in contact. He now said,—

"Mr. Davis, the space between the extremities of this tendon is very small, consequently there is so much less new matter to be formed. You will not suffer much pain, but you will sustain a great trial of your patience, more than though your leg was broken, for then you would feel compelled to lie still. The rapidity and thoroughness of your cure will be in proportion to the patience you exercise, and the degree of care you take in respect to those motions absolutely necessary. It will be six weeks or more before this new substance I have been speaking of will form between the ends, and many months before you can place much strain upon the tendon."

"Shall I have to lie in bed long?"

"No; but you must keep perfectly still for a while. You will not be able to wear this splint long. It is only extemporized for the occasion. I'll make something better to-morrow."

The second day, after school hours, Richardson visited his patient again, and directed Mrs. Davis to make a shoe of carpeting, slipper-fashion, leaving the toe a little open, to prevent galling, and sewing a strap to the heel of it. This he fastened to a bandage around the leg above the calf, which took the place of the splint, kept the heel back, the foot forward, and the ends of the tendon in their place, and was much more comfortable for the patient.

Farmer Davis in eight weeks was relieved from the slipper, strap, and bandage during the night, putting them on in the daytime, and began to walk with a cane. There was a bunch on the tendon the size of a robin's egg, which gradually disappeared; and in four months the limb was as serviceable as ever.

When, a fortnight after the event, Dr. Ryan ascertained that Rich had merely brought the ends of the tendon within half an inch, and let it go at that, he shook his head, looked anxious, but said nothing. Dr. Slaughter was not so reticent, and declared the parts would never unite, but grow to the sheath, and the man be lame for life.

Richardson now pursued the even tenor of his way, without the least interruption till the middle of the winter, when he was called to old Mr. Avery, a shingle weaver, who had cut himself with his draw-shave. The wound bled a great deal before Richardson arrived, and the patient being an old man, it healed very slowly. Avery became impatient, and thought his physician was not doing enough. Rich, unable to convince him, as he was a very ignorant and obstinate man, that the process of healing must necessarily be slow, on account of his age, and that nature must do the work, called in Dr. Ryan, who confirmed the judgment of Rich and approved his method, but the patient not convinced, fussed and fretted, said Rich "was *doing nothing*," and talked about "sending for Dr. Slaughter." Rich, at his wits' end, and not relishing the idea of having a patient taken out of his hands, cast about for some way of keeping him quiet.

At length, in a wakeful hour of the night, he bethought himself of a means of relief, suggested by something he had read in one of the old romances while in college, and the next day proceeded to put it in practice.

"Mr. Avery," he said, "I think I have discovered something that will be just the thing you need, and answer the purpose completely."

"Do let me know it, then, right off. I ought to be at work in the shop this minute."

"Do you think the draw-shave that you cut yourself with has been used since? Because if it has, nothing can be done, and the charm will be broken."

"No, I know it 'tain't; 'cause I laid it across the horse, and the shop's been locked up ever sence. Then you can charm; that's something like. There was a woman in this town could charm; but she died four year ago; and she didn't give her power to anybody. They say they kin, if they like, give it to anybody else, that is, if they're a seventh son or darter, not without."

"You don't believe that nonsense, I hope."

"Sartain sure I do. I *know* that woman could charm. But you doctors never believe anything you don't do yourselves, or don't read in a book; but that's nuther here nor there. What is it you've found out?"

"Well, Mr. Avery, the ancient wise folks, a great many hundred years ago, had a custom of applying the rust of the weapon or tool that made the wound to it; or, if there was no rust, of making the applications to the instrument; and by some secret, mysterious influence, as they held, the wound was healed."

"There, now, that stan's to reason. You've said somethin' to the p'int now. I believe in them ere things what's handed down from the old forefathers. I tell you they forgot more'n we ever knew. These things what's handed down, they're sperience, they ain't guesswork. The Indians can cure cancers, but the white doctors can't. Mercy Jane, you git the key out of my westcoat pocket, and bring in that ere draw-shave; it's laying across the horse."

When the draw-shave was brought; to the great satisfaction both of Rich and his patient, considerable rust was found on the edge. Avery had ground it the afternoon he cut himself, and only drawn a few strokes before he inflicted the wound, and the water from the grinding, still on the edge, caused it, after lying, to rust. Rich, carefully scraping the rust from the tool (about enough to cover the point of a penknife), applied it to the wound. He next produced several large plasters of different colors, red, black, green, blue, and yellow.

"What are them plasters spread with?" said the patient.

"Indeed, Mr. Avery, that is an affair of my own."

"I'll warrant it. That's allers the way with doctors."

"Neither will I apply it, or go one step farther, unless you will solemnly promise me that you will observe strictly my directions as to diet, and stay in your bed or your chair, and keep the limb still."

"Well, I will, I sartainly will. I'll do jist zactly as you tell me to."

"See that you don't forget it the moment I am out of the room; if you do, it will be the worse for you, that's all, for those are plasters of tremendous power, and if you do not, you will have something horribilis, aspectu horridus, detestabilis, abominandus."

Rich held up his hands in horror and made an awful face. They were indeed of tremendous power, and had they been applied to his flesh instead of to the draw-shave, would soon have put him beyond the cares and trials of this stormy life. One, the green, was made of hog's lard, beef tallow, and verdigris; the blue, of beeswax, linseed oil, and Prussian blue; the black, of the same materials, colored with lampblack; the red, with vermilion, a mercurial compound, quicksilver, and sulphur; and the yellow with gamboge. Rich now produced several large rolls of bandages, and, after strewing the plasters with brick dust, applied them to the knife, and then enveloped the whole in fold over fold of the bandage, till the knife was as large as a man's thigh.

"Now," he said to Mrs. Avery, "this must be put where no rat, mouse, cat, or any other creature can get at it."

"I'm sure," said she, "I don't know of any safer place than the oven. We've got two; and one I don't use often."

"Well, put it in the oven."

After Rich left, Avery said,—

"Wife, Mr. Richardson knows a lot; he'll make a great doctor."

"I expect he will. But, husband, you must keep still, and do jist as he told you, and mustn't hanker after pork and beans. You know what he said—'if you didn't, it would be worser for you.' And what them awful outlandish words meant I don't know; but I expect they meant you'd die right off if you didn't do everything jist as he said."

"Well, I mean to keep as still as a mouse. You must tell me when I don't."

When Rich again visited his patient, he said,—

"Mr. Avery, there has been a very marked improvement in your leg, and it will soon be well, if you continue to follow implicitly my directions."

"I knew that would do the business. It begun to feel better the minute you put them ere plasters on to the draw-shave."

In a short time it was well; and, lest our young readers should attribute the cure to the wrong means, we would say that, Mr. Avery being in years, his flesh healed slowly, and, as he was of a nervous temperament, kept irritating his wound all the time by motion, and refused to govern his appetite. This conduct aggravated the difficulty. Whereas his faith in the strange remedy appealing to the superstitious sentiments of his nature, and fear of the terrible consequences couched under the Latin of Rich, kept him quiet, and effected the cure by giving nature time to operate.

Rich had now accumulated a little money, and resolved to visit his patients, attend medical lectures at Brunswick, and see Morton on his way. He accordingly employed Perk to finish out the term, as part of the period of his absence would be during the vacation. As his funds were by no means excessive, he made the journey on foot, with the exception of a few miles of the first part of the way, over which he was carried by Dan Clemens.

It was near night on the second day, and Rich, weary, hungry, and foot-sore, had been for some time expecting to come in sight of a village where was a tavern; but none appeared. At length his patience was exhausted, and arriving at a substantial-looking farm-house, he knocked, and inquired of the farmer, who came at the summons, how far it was to the next tavern.

"Well, 'tis good three miles; yes, strong that." But noticing the disappointed look of Rich, said, "Young man, you look tired. If you'll stop with me, you shall be welcome to such as we have."

Rich gladly accepted the invitation, and was ushered into the kitchen, where he found the farmer's family, consisting of his wife, two sons, and two daughters. One of the daughters immediately rose, pulled the table into the floor, put on the tea-kettle, and, as Rich thought (who was very hungry, for he had eaten since morning only a luncheon), provided a meal about as speedily as he had ever seen it done in his life.

"My mother," thought he, "couldn't do better than that."

Rich was at first surprised that neither the mother nor elder sister gave any assistance to this young woman in preparing an extra meal, but continued their sewing. He afterwards, however, ascertained that the thrifty mother brought up her daughters to take their week around in the kitchen doing the cooking; and that it was this daughter's week. After making ready for Rich, she began to iron at a table in the corner of the room, and when he finished, cleared away the dishes, and resumed her ironing. He was very much struck with the domestic accomplishments of the young woman, and thought her extremely good-looking; but this might be owing to the fact, that, being very hungry, he felt grateful for a bountiful meal so speedily provided; his habits of thought as a physician also led him to notice that she was well-formed and in fine health.

His boots off, seated before a cheerful fire, and well fed, Rich forgot his fatigue, and passed a most pleasant evening. He endeavored several times to draw into conversation Miss Caroline; but she stuck to her ironing, and merely replied to his questions politely.

At bed-time he said to the farmer,—

"Mr. Conant, I will settle with you before I go to bed, as I mean to start by sunrise."

"But you will not start on a day's walk without breakfast."

"I will get my breakfast at the next village. That will divide the forenoon about right; and after walking three miles I shall be 'sharp set' for eating."

"Mr. Richardson, I can contrive better than that. I shan't take a cent for your keeping, and William will put the horse in the sleigh and take you to the village. He was going to start early to carry something to market there. You will have your breakfast, and be well started on your journey, and when you come back, make it in your way to call here. We shall be right pleased to see you. I'll give you a lift on your way."

The next morning Rich was up by break of day, and found that William had harnessed the horse, and Caroline had the breakfast ready. He now found her rather less reserved, and went away with a most favorable impression of her intelligence.

After a very delightful visit at home, where he found everything pleasant and prosperous, his parents on the original homestead, with every prospect of soon owning it, seeing Morton and enjoying a glorious time with him, by some singular combination of circumstances he was again overtaken by night at farmer Conant's door when it never looked more like a storm, which indeed came that night, and Rich was obliged to stay there two days, which, however, passed very pleasantly.

CHAPTER XXIII.
THE TURN OF THE TIDE.

When Rich returned, shortly after the commencement of the summer term, he was joyfully welcomed by his pupils. In the course of ten days he received a box by the stage, of quite modest proportions, that was instantly transferred to the harness-room, and respecting the reception of which Rich seemed very much interested, having been several times to the stage tavern to inquire about it.

This box contained all the bones of the human frame; and no wonder that Rich was concerned about their arrival, considering his intense interest in the study of anatomy, and furthermore, the low state of his funds, and that they cost him but five dollars.

It was customary for the lecturer to procure subjects for dissection (in what way was best known to himself), for any students who wished this opportunity of private study and dissection, at twenty dollars apiece. Rich clubbed with three more and bought one. After they had dissected and made a study of the different parts in which each felt most specially interested, the bones remained. To secure and put these together properly, so as to form an entire and perfect skeleton, repairing the damages made by the dissecting saw on the skull, to get at the brain, was a great deal of work, and required not only anatomical knowledge, but great patience and no small degree of mechanical skill; and the other students, who were able to purchase skeletons already prepared, and possessed neither the patience nor mechanical ability to perform the work, and, moreover, liked Rich, gave him their portion of the bones.

To prepare, classify, and wire them together was a most congenial as well as profitable occupation to Rich; it fixed the arrangement, names, and shape of the bones and articulations in his mind, and also gratified his mechanical tastes; and he in the course of the summer accomplished the work, during the performance of which his practice in working iron stood him in good stead, as he replaced the spinal marrow by an iron rod, cut a thread on each end, and made thumb-nuts with which to confine the vertebral column.

The fact of his having attended medical lectures at Brunswick, coupled with his previous success in some cases of minor importance, increased very much the confidence of people in general touching his ability as a physician, and he had numerous calls, to all of which he turned a deaf ear, devoting himself entirely to his scholars and studies.

At length circumstances concurred to place him in a position of great perplexity, and one where he was, as it were, compelled to assume a responsibility from which he would gladly have been excused. Dan Clemens, Frank Merrill, and Horace Williams had natural history, in the form of ornithology, "on the brain." If these youngsters didn't sit on eggs, they dreamed of them. It would be difficult to mention anything they would not do for Rich when the remuneration was a *rare bird*, shot and stuffed.

To be soaked to the skin, and so tired they could scarcely put one foot before the other, were pastimes when birds were ahead; and to obtain eggs they would venture life and limb. The fatigue of soldiers on a forced march was trifling in comparison with what they cheerfully endured; and their mothers, during the spring and summer months, were in a state of chronic anxiety, expecting nothing less than their being brought home with broken bones.

One Saturday afternoon they were all in swimming with a crowd of boys who took not the least interest in their favorite study; but one of them, while undressing under a leafy elm, at whose roots the boys were accustomed to put their clothes, espied the nest of a Baltimore oriole, and told Dan, who was in the water with Frank and Horace. They instantly dressed, and began to look with longing eyes at the nest that was pendent from the extremity of a slender branch near the top of the tree, and on its southern side.

"We can't get that nest," said Horace, "for we can't climb the tree, it's so far to a limb. If we could climb it, the limbs won't bear a fellow to reach the nest."

"Yes, we can," said Dan; "we must have those eggs. You give me a boost. I'll bet I can climb it."

"If you do, you can't reach the nest."

"I can tell better after I get there."

Dan did his best, but had to give it up; so did Horace. Frank was the best climber of the three, though of lighter weight than the others, and less plump—an exceedingly agile and sinewy boy. He did not, however, relinquish his efforts and slide reluctantly down the trunk till he was within three feet of the lowest limb.

"If you could only boost me up that much I fell short, I could go it," said Frank, "after I rest and get breath."

"Let us," said Dan, "pile up a great heap of stones, one of us stand on that, and the rest put Frank's feet on his shoulders."

"No; get some nails and a hammer, and nail some pieces of board on the tree," said Horace.

"Zuckers! I know how you can git up," said a barefooted, red-headed boy of twelve, whose hat-rim was nearly torn off thrashing bumblebees on thistle blossoms, and who didn't go to the academy nor any other school, save a few weeks in the winter, and who lived on a farm three miles from the village, but had the presumption to come there and go in swimming with the academy boys, because it was the best place on the river, and who could swim like a fish.

"You shut up," said Frank. "How much do *you* know about it? And what business have *you* there in *our* swimming-place?"

"Tain't none of *your* place, nuther; it's Mr. Seth Hardin's pastur. I've good right here's you have. If you touch me, I'll heave a stone at your head, and I'll tell our Sam, and he'll give you a lickin'."

"What is the way, bub?" said Dan, too anxious to get the eggs to fling away any chance of success. "What do you know about it?"

"I know our Sam would git up that tree quick as a cat would lick her ear, I swanny."

"How, bub?"

"Arter plantin', dad allers gives Sam half a day to go troutin' and git elum rine (elm rind) to string our corn, and me and Abigail allers go too. Sam takes the axe and starts a strip of bark at the butt of a tree, till he can git his hands hold; then he gives it a twitch, and rips it up clear to the limbs; then he starts another one till he gits enough. Arter that he takes hold of one on 'em, and climbs up jist like nothin', and cuts 'em all off but one rope that he saves to come down on. They break off sometimes when there's a knot-hole; they won't run over a knot-hole. Abigail and me has jolly times swingin' on the ropes afore he cuts 'em off, and strippin' 'em into twine arter he takes the outside bark off, and windin' 'em into big balls."

The inner bark of the elm, cedar, bass, and willow is very strong and tough; when peeled from the outside layer and soaked in water it makes a very good substitute for twine. Our ancestors were taught the value of it by the Indians, and used it to string their corn and bind sheaves, and some old-fashioned people have not yet abandoned the practice. Getting elm rind and cutting withe rods were always popular with the boys, as it gave them part of a holiday.

"That's it," said Dan; "I see it all now. Here, bub."

He gave him three cents, upon which little Red-head put his bare feet to the ground and went off at a killing pace.

An axe was procured at Seth Harding's, and a strip of bark peeled from the butt of the tree to one of the lower limbs.

"Let us all go up," said Horace. "We will stay in the tree and take the nest from Frank. He's the lightest to go out on the limb."

Frank, taking hold of the piece of bark, put his legs around the tree, and pulled himself up, ascending in this way quite easily. Too impatient to wait, Dan and Horace followed suit, all three ascending at the same time.

In their haste and anxiety to run the bark as far up as possible, in order to reach one of the lower limbs easily, they ran it too far, within a few inches of the place where the branch joined the tree. The result of this was, that when they were pretty well up the trunk, Frank incautiously pressing the bark from the tree with his knees, it started the second time and ran out on the limb. Away swung the boys, far off from the trunk, in mid-air. The bark kept running narrower and narrower, as the limb grew smaller, till, its farther progress being suddenly arrested by a number of small limbs, it divided up and broke, while the boys came down into the water, amid the shouts and laughter of the rest, who were either swimming or putting on their clothes.

A SLIPPERY ELM. Page 266.

Frank escaped without hurt, but he gave Dan a bloody nose with the heels of his shoes, while Horace, who was undermost, barked both shins on a rock that just broke the surface of the water.

Learning wisdom from experience, they stripped the bark at the next trial farther from the limb, ascending one at a time, and met with no difficulty. The branch on which the nest hung bent over the river. Frank, grasping the branch, put his feet on the one directly beneath it, and thus gradually worked his way till he came very near the nest, and the parent birds began to fly around his head.

But the branch now bent so much that Dan, who had been the most anxious to obtain the nest and its contents, begged him to desist and give it up; so did Horace; but Frank's blood was up and his pride roused, for there was a crowd of boys looking at him.

"If I fall," he said, "I shall fall into the water, and I can swim ashore."

At length he could touch the outside of the nest with the tips of his fingers.

"O, if my arm was only two inches longer!"

"Don't, Frank," said Dan, "go any farther. It frightens me to see the limb bend so."

Scarcely were the words uttered, when the limb upon which he stood broke as he was holding to the branch above by only one hand. Reaching after the nest with the other, he fell feet foremost into the river, catching by the limbs as he went. There were boys still in the water, who, instantly swam to him, while Dan and Horace, hurrying down the tree, plunged in. Frank kept himself on top of the water, after rising, but when the boys reached him, said,—

"I can't swim; I believe my leg is broke. I struck something under water, and heard it snap."

It was on a Saturday afternoon that this accident occurred, and Rich had embraced the opportunity to work upon his bones. He was busily engaged in the harness-room, with the door fastened, when he was startled by a rousing rap, and the voice of Dan clamoring for admittance. Opening the door, he beheld Dan pale and excited, and the face of Mrs. Clemens over his shoulder, who manifested no less alarm.

"O, Mr. Richardson!" cried Dan, "Frank's fell off a tree and broke his leg. Horace and Mr. Harding have carried him home, and Dr. Ryan has gone down there, and wants you to come right down. Mr. Harding said be expected they'd cut his leg off. Mr. Richardson, don't let 'em cut poor Frank's leg off—will you?"

"I hope it won't be necessary," said Rich, as he locked the door; "but the doctors will do what they think is for the best."

"Just what I have been expecting all the spring, ever since this egg-hunting began. I hope it will be a solemn warning to you, Daniel," said his mother.

It happened very opportunely that this was a day fixed upon by Dr. Ryan and his friend, Dr. Slaughter, to remove a tumor, the person being one of Dr.

Ryan's patients. They had returned, having performed the operation, and were at the house in a few moments after the boy was brought home, and Richardson was not far behind them.

"You had better strip the limb, Mr. Richardson," said Dr. Ryan; "he is more familiar with you."

Rich bared the leg by ripping the clothes at the seam, and the two physicians commenced their examination. In his fall the boy had struck on the end of a sunken log, the remaining portion being imbedded in the bank, and both bones were broken. The tibia (or larger bone) was fractured obliquely, the sharp point of the upper end protruding through the skin; and the fibula (or smaller bone) probably with a pipe-stem fracture (square across.)

The physicians now went into a room apart for consultation, and Rich, whom they did not invite to accompany them, employed himself in examining the leg, and endeavoring to soothe and encourage the boy.

Dr. Slaughter gave it as his opinion, that the limb must be amputated at once.

Dr. Ryan shrank from this, referred to the age and firm constitution of the patient, thought "it was a pity that the boy should be made a cripple at his time of life; that, though one of the fractures was oblique, the bone was not comminuted, and hoped it might be set, and the patient do well."

His brother physician, on the other hand, was positive.

"It was a compound fracture, and it was a settled principle in anatomy always to amputate in a compound fracture. Air had been admitted, the muscles and integuments lacerated and bruised; mortification would take place, the leg would have to be amputated higher up after all, with scarcely a chance for life."

Dr. Ryan, accustomed for years to look to his companion for direction in all surgical operations, was obliged to yield the point; and the parents were informed it was the opinion of the physicians that amputation was necessary. Mr. Merrill, who reposed the greatest confidence in Dr. Ryan, and was not aware that he had hesitated in the matter, acquiesced at once, though with tears, for Frank was their only child.

But it was very different with the mother, who was a woman of excellent judgment, great penetration, and decision of character. She utterly refused, divined that Dr. Ryan secretly cherished a different opinion and did not act freely, and entreated the physicians to set the bones, and bind up the wound. But this Dr. Slaughter refused to do. They then informed their son of the doctors' decision.

"Mother," said Frank, "I had rather die than have my leg cut off, and be a cripple for life."

They then asked the opinion of Rich, but he declined to advance any.

"Well, wife," said the husband, "we must say something; the doctors are waiting. I'll do as you think best."

"I," replied she, firmly, "will not give my consent to amputation."

"Well, abide the consequences, then," said Dr. Slaughter; and he left the house in a huff, followed reluctantly by his companion and Richardson.

The parents looked at each other, after they had gone, in doubt and dread. There lay the boy, nothing done as yet, and every moment of delay, increasing the difficulty of cure and augmenting the danger.

"Shall I harness up, wife, and go to B. after Dr. Loring, or to M. after Dr. Blake?"

"They will probably refuse to do anything but amputate. No, husband. Let us send for Mr. Richardson."

"O, do, mother," said Frank; "he's better than all the other doctors in this world, and he loves me."

"It is not likely he would do anything," replied the father. "We asked his opinion, and he wouldn't give any."

"To be sure he wouldn't before them. I know that he didn't think the limb ought to be taken off—saw it in his looks. I don't believe Dr. Ryan did, either, only Dr. Slaughter has got him under his thumb."

Rich was eating his supper when Mr. Merrill came for him, and shoving back his plate, went with him directly.

"Mr. Richardson," said the mother, "there is no one here but ourselves. Please to speak freely. Do you think it is necessary or best to cut off Frank's leg?"

"I do not. I think there is as great a chance for the boy to live with the limb on as off—that the bones may be set, and the limb saved as good as ever."

"Will you give me your reasons, and tell me what Dr. Slaughter meant by a compound fracture, and why doctors always amputate in that case; and do it in language that his father and I can understand?"

"A simple fracture is where the bones are broken, but there is no external wound, and when the bones are set they heal for the most part readily. But a compound fracture is one in which the bone pushes through the skin, the muscles are lacerated, or, by the agent that breaks the bone, an external wound made, and air admitted. The laceration of the muscles and the admission of air, especially the presence of air, causes inflammation, the wound suppurates, sloughs, instead of healing, and ulceration is produced; it then becomes necessary to amputate, and the patient, being reduced, often dies. The old physicians thought less of saving the limb than the modern ones, and in case of compound fracture always amputated."

"Is not this a compound fracture?"

"It must be defined as such technically. But the muscles are not lacerated; and though the bone protrudes, I have not the least doubt that it was done by the sharp point of the bone pricking through in consequence of the foot's falling back when they took him up, and that it was not forced through by the violence of the blow. It is therefore so near to a simple fracture that it may be considered and treated as one, with a fair chance of success, especially considering the patient's age, health, and the time of year (for the weather is not hot as yet), and that he is at home, where he will have the best of nursing."

"Mr. Richardson," said the father, "I know in these matters the state of a patient's mind has much to do with the final results. The boy will not submit to amputation except by compulsion. That we cannot think of. But he loves you, and has the most perfect confidence in your ability. Will you set the bones, and do as you think best?"

"Mr. Merrill, I am a young man, without experience to guide me. I have no guide other than what I have gathered from books, a few weeks' instruction, and practice of dissection at Brunswick, and my own unmatured judgment; but I also know that before you can get a physician here from another town, swelling will take place, and the chance of recovery be greatly diminished. I will do it on condition that you take upon yourselves all the responsibility. If a regular physician should amputate the limb, and the result be unfavorable, it would be said he took the regular steps; he would have the authority of precedent, and the approval of other physicians; and the ill success would be attributed to the providence of God; whereas in my case it would be said, 'He is a rash, ignorant upstart and pretender, puffed up with conceit to trifle with human life.' It would destroy confidence in me for the future, and prove a poor introduction to practice."

"We will do that, and, moreover, make it public, let the event be what it may."

Rich now manifested as much despatch as he had previously displayed reluctance.

"Frank," he said, "I shall be obliged to give you some pain, but I will not do it unnecessarily, nor to any great extent."

The bone completely filled the wound it had made, the point protruding slightly, and a little blood trickled down the leg from a slight flesh wound in the upper part of the thigh. Rich in the first place removed the protruding point of ragged bone with the saw, and then, dipping a bunch of lint in the blood that issued from the flesh wound, gave it to Dan to hold. He then gently returned the bone, Dan applying the lint, and lightly pressing it to the wound as the bone receded. Rich then applied a sticking plaster, spread only at the edges, over the whole, sponged, and bound up the flesh wound. Thus, no air having been admitted to the wound, the fracture, in that respect, and on account of the absence of laceration, might be considered as virtually a simple one. Then, with the aid of assistants, he flexed the thigh on the abdomen and the leg on the thigh, thus relaxing the muscles, by which he was enabled to put the bones in place, and, retaining them with his hands, brought the leg gently down and straightened it.

One assistant, now taking hold of the heel, extended the leg, while another held the thigh, and Rich manipulated the ends of the bones. By bringing the heels and toes of both feet in line, and sighting across, they assured themselves that the legs were of equal length, and the foot in the right position; that there was no twist, no turning of the foot out or in. He then applied the splints, and, in order to preserve extension, by reason of the contraction of the muscles, put a shoe on the foot and attached half of a brick to it with a string. It requires a good deal of force to counteract the contraction of a muscle, if exerted at once, but much less when applied gradually and constantly.

Although progress was now the watchword among the younger portion of the medical fraternity, and a decided improvement had been made in surgical instruments, still very few of the appliances now in common use were then known in this country (starch and plaster of Paris, and dextrine bandages for broken bones, fracture-beds and boxes, cutting-forceps to remove bone, &c.,) and Richardson could not have obtained them if they had been, and, like his grandfather, under the stimulus of a determined purpose, invented the appliances he felt to be needful.

"It's all over now, Frank," said Rich, sitting down by him and patting his cheek; "the leg is set, and you have borne it like a hero. Remember you are *my* boy after this, and when your leg gets well I shall expect you to run all my errands. This dressing is only temporary, because the limb will swell, and the bandages perhaps, require to be loosened. It will be five or six days before the bones will begin to knit, and then I shall put on a permanent fixture. I am going to take care of you myself to-night, as to-morrow is Sunday, no school, and I can sleep. After that I must be in school."

Having requested the family to retire, he placed the light in the next room, administered a sedative to the patient, and resumed his seat beside him. Never had Rich such cause for anxiety before. In addition to his affection for the lad, who was in truth a noble-minded, lovable boy, he felt that he had ventured upon an innovation in surgical practice, and taken a bold step, which success alone could justify. The confidence reposed in him by the parents in thus placing their only child in his hands touched him to the quick, and he felt that it was with him the turning-point, the decisive step in professional life.

Kneeling down by the bedside, he offered a heartfelt petition to God for direction and support.

"Mr. Richardson," said Frank.

"What is it, my boy?"

"I begin to feel drowsy, and my leg don't pain me much. I want to kiss you before I go to sleep."

Rich bent over him, and the grateful boy, putting his arms around his teacher's neck, kissed him, and dropped asleep.

CHAPTER XXIV.
THE YOUNG FLOOD.

Two or three times before midnight Frank started spasmodically, and once would have risen up in bed if Rich had not held him down; as it was, he clasped his physician convulsively around the neck with great force.

"What is the matter, Frank?"

"I thought I was falling out of the tree. I suppose I was dreaming."

In one respect Rich was favorably situated. He had but one patient, and every moment he could spare from his school he either spent at the bedside of the boy, or in studying his case by the aid of books; he availed himself of the experience of Dr. Ryan, who knew the constitution of the lad, sympathized with Rich, and, in the exercise of a noble generosity, told him he was glad he had taken charge of the case, and believed he would succeed.

The means resorted to by Rich to prevent inflammation were crowned with success; the swelling of the muscles, never excessive, soon subsided, and he found the wound was healing by the first intention, which far exceeded his most sanguine hopes, as he feared some air might have entered, or some splinter of bone be lying loose in the wound that would cause suppuration.

It was time for new bone to begin to form, and consequently the shape the limb now assumed it would retain through life. Rich knew several persons in town whose limbs had been broken and set by Dr. Ryan, and he could hardly recall a single instance in which the operation had been entirely successful; nearly all walked with a hitch in their gait, many used a staff, or wore a peculiarly-shaped shoe. He also noticed that most of the persons thus partially crippled lived at a long distance from Dr. Ryan, and concluded that it arose in a good degree either from a mistaken economy on the part of the patient, anxious to save the cost of a visit, or from careless bandaging on the part of the doctor.

Excited to the highest degree by the brilliant success thus far attained, and knowledge that the boy's life was safe, he longed, O, how ardently! to make a *perfect* cure, and restore the leg to its original form and efficiency.

He reflected that less discretion and regard to future consequences were to be expected from a lad like Frank than from a grown person; didn't feel satisfied with the old splints, was afraid that, unless he bandaged the leg so tight as to impede the circulation, the restless boy would, just at the critical period when the bone was forming, get the parts out of place.

"I know," said Rich to himself, "that I am mechanic enough to *place* those bones as they should be, and I'll see if I cannot contrive some way to *keep* them there in spite of this wide-awake youngster."

He went to bed in order to think about it, and in the morning at the breakfast table said to Mrs. Clemens,—

"Where did you get that blue clay the girl was putting on the floor yesterday to take out a grease-spot? It had no more grit than tailors'-chalk."

"Daniel got it somewhere."

"I got it down in Milliken's Gully, Mr. Richardson. You might cut it with a razor, and not dull the razor; there's not a stone or one mite of grit in it. I got it to make marbles."

Richardson procured a quantity of the clay, dried, pounded, sifted, and made it into a very thin mortar. He then took the splints from Frank's leg, placed the bones precisely as he wanted them, put the leg in a box, fastened the upper portion of his body to the bed that he could not move, and poured the clay mortar into the box till it completely enveloped the leg and foot. He then pulled the bed under the window, where the sun shone full on the clay, took hold of Frank's foot, and sat down.

"How long are you going to keep me lashed down so, Mr. Richardson?"

"Till this clay dries. And I shall hold your foot just where it is till then."

"Why, Mr. Richardson," said Mrs. Merrill, "it will take all day for that clay to dry."

"No, it won't, with the warmth of the leg on one side, and that of the sun on the other, it won't take *half* a day."

"But the academy bell will ring in about fifteen minutes."

"Parson Meek is going to take my place this forenoon; so you may prepare to give me some dinner, for I shall sit here till the clay hardens, if it is till to-morrow evening."

The clay was stiff, though not dry, before noon, and Frank's leg immovably fixed in the position Rich had placed it.

"Now, Frank, you have behaved so well, I am going to put you in a chair."

Rich and Mr. Merrill took Frank up, placed him in a chair, and put the leg, box and all, on two others.

"Now, my boy, you may sit at the table and eat dinner with us, if you will eat only what I prescribe; and you may thank the blue clay in Milliken's Gully for that. Blue clay, forever, Frank. Were it not for that you would have had to lie on your back twenty days or more."

After the meal was ended, Rich, with a saw, cut out a portion of the clay, in order to be able to get at that part of the leg the bone had penetrated. The box was also lined with paper, that the clay might not stick to it, and put together with screws, in order that it might be taken to pieces. This was Rich's fracture box, not very elegant, and for which he never took out any patent; being made, the sides, of the cover of an old herring box; but it answered the purpose completely, fastening the limb as firmly in the box as though it grew there, and as effectually preventing any motion of the ankle or toes, by which the bones might be displaced.

When Rich went to the academy in the afternoon, he returned Frank to his bed; and the next morning he was taken up again, and, as the cure progressed, sat up more and more. He could now read, play checkers with Dan and Horace, and the time passed less tediously. He now importuned his physician to take his leg out of the box; but Rich peremptorily refused, though he allowed him a more generous diet.

When a full month had elapsed, Rich took the box apart, sawed through the coating of clay the whole length, and peeled it off, removed the bandage, washed the leg, gave it a smart rubbing, and compared it with the other. After examining the limb a long time very carefully, he said,—

"If those two legs are not as well matched as they were before, I am very much mistaken."

"Shall I be lame any, Mr. Richardson?" said Frank.

"If you are, it will be your own fault. If you are careless now, you will rue it as long as you live, for the parts are not consolidated yet, and the oblique fracture in the large bone requires a longer time to heal than the square break in the other."

Rich put on the clay again, but without the box, and in less quantity, confining it by a bandage, slung the patient's leg to his neck, and permitted him to take exercise by walking about the house on crutches, some one accompanying him; and when he permitted him to put his injured leg to the floor, it was found to be of the same length as the other.

Mr. Merrill rewarded Rich most liberally, being abundantly able, and with expressions of grateful feeling that were more gratifying to the recipient than even the money. It was a proud and glad morning to him when Frank Merrill came to school with his books under his arm, escorted by Dan and Horace Williams, and with as firm a tread as his companions.

Scarcely had Frank's case been disposed of, when a younger sister of Mrs. Merrill, a member of the choir, and a most lovely girl as far as personal attractions, correct principles, and amiability of disposition went, was taken down with a lung fever; and the patient, with her parents and Mrs. Merrill, insisted that Rich should manage the case. This was more practice than Rich either desired or felt himself qualified to assume, and he told them so, and that he should pursue quite a different method from the ordinary practice, which was, in that disease, to bleed patients till they fainted, give them antimony to reduce the action of the heart, till, in reducing the inflammation, they often made an end of the patient. The young lady's relatives informed him they were not at all concerned about that, and to adopt the course his judgment dictated. In so doing, Rich drew no blood, and pursued a course calculated to support the strength of the patient as much as possible, and was successful in this case also.

At the conclusion of the summer term Rich resolved to make another visit to his parents, but felt that in his present circumstances he could afford to ride; and, what was very singular, he spent a night at farmer Conant's, taking the stage from his door the next afternoon. It certainly could not have been from fatigue, as on the former occasion. It was probably to thank the hospitable farmer for his kindness then, and it was a noble thing in Rich not to forget, in the moment of success, those who had been his friends in adversity.

With the fall term commenced another year of the academical course, when it was necessary for Rich to make a new arrangement with the trustees, who were very anxious to retain him, and offered to increase his salary. On the other hand, Dr. Ryan wanted him to give up the academy, devote himself entirely to the study of medicine, obtain a medical diploma, go into practice with him and finally take his place, as he did not care to practise any more.

The doctor said he loved him as a son, and that if he did not improve the opening, some other young man would certainly come who might be very objectionable.

Rich replied that he would at the expiration of two years, and then agreed to keep the academy one year longer; thus affording himself a year of uninterrupted study, in addition to what he could accomplish while teaching, and resolutely refused all invitations to take charge of patients.

The fall term had been going on but a week when he received a visit from Morton. The inhabitants of the village showed great attention to Morton, as a compliment to Rich, and especially Mr. Merrill's family, and that of Mr.

George Litchfield, the father of the young lady Rich had attended during a course of lung fever.

As the two friends were walking one evening, Morton said,—

"Rich, why don't you make up to that Miss Litchfield? She's a beautiful girl, intelligent, accomplished, and of most amiable disposition, I know, for she shows it in her very looks. You are about to jump into a fat practice, that will give you a handsome living at once, and it is time you were thinking of such matters. I know she likes you, and her father is wealthy, which, though I know it would weigh little with you, is not to be despised."

"Mort, why did not you take Miss T., whom you used to like to escort to exhibitions and commencements, and walk with, and who was more beautiful than Harriet Litchfield, and in preference engaged yourself to Eliza Longley?"

"Because I wanted a wife, not a doll, a woman who would make for me a happy home."

"Now you have answered your own question. Miss Litchfield is beautiful and of a sweet temper, for I have seen her when sick, and sickness developes character. She is well educated, sings finely, plays well, is not vain, and is sincerely pious, but has neither industry, energy, nor a single domestic trait. She cannot make or mend, get a meal's victuals, or tell anybody else how to do it. Her counsel in the emergencies of life, which you and I have known something about even at our age, would not be worth the asking. Why, Mort, she is as hollow as the stalk of a seed onion; no resources in herself, and for all the practical duties of life utterly useless. How could I respect a woman who, if she has not a piano to amuse, or some gossip to engage her attention, sits and folds her hands, and resembles a wooden clock, the face the best part of it? You saw how my mother stood up under the load, and took her share of it, when father's property was swept into the Atlantic; and it will be a long day before a boy who has such a mother marries a doll."

"I rather think, Rich, such a woman as you want is not easily found."

"Neither are diamonds. But you found such a one, and so have I."

"Indeed! I congratulate you. But who and where is she? Is she handsome?"

"She is not beautiful, but as handsome as good health, regular features, and a perfect form can render a woman."

"Is she accomplished?"

"To the highest degree. She can spin and weave, wash and mend, make butter, and make clothes; and when she's tired, or has a leisure hour, can sit down and obtain both profit and pleasure from a thoughtful book."

"It is little you would have thought of falling in love with such a woman when we first knew each other. What has become of all the poetry that was in you then, and, I had almost said, the froth on the top of the liquor?"

"It went to sea when the boom broke."

"I long to see her."

"You shall Sunday, and eat a dinner of her cooking. We will ride over there Saturday. She is a farmer's daughter. There is no *property* in the matter, of the kind you referred to just now. It is all in *her*."

"You know what I told you, Rich, so long ago, when we were sitting on the steps of your old house, and the cat shoved her nose into your bosom. It was dead *low water* then; but now the tide has not only turned, but it is young flood, and the tide will continue to flow till, at high water it will lift the strawberry leaves on the edge of the bank."

"True, Mort; but I do not regret the trial. I have gained more than I lost by it. Have you heard anything from college lately, or from our old class?"

"No. All our acquaintances are gone, and there is a new set in Radcliffe. But they are only going to keep it during the fall term; after that it is to be made into a dwelling-house. Charlie Longley wrote me that the dam at the Glen had washed away in the fall rains, and the pond had run out."

Their conversation was interrupted by meeting Dr. Ryan, who invited them to go home with him, enjoy a sing, and take tea.

The next volume of the series is entitled, A STOUT HEART, OR, THE STUDENT FROM OVER THE SEA.

Milton Keynes UK
Ingram Content Group UK Ltd.
UKHW020828231024
450026UK00004B/453